JULIA

From the moment he meets Julia, Christaan Dudok is dangerously close to love. But their first date is interrupted by S.A. Brownshirts storming into the café. It is 1938, and Germany is heading for war and fanaticism. Chris, a Dutchman, is both transfixed and appalled by the effect of Hitler's manic oratory on the people of Lübeck. The independence and freedom of thought that Chris finds so attractive in Julia lead her to emphatically reject the Nazi regime, and before long her courageous stance brings them both to the Gestapo's attention. Soon Chris is forced to make an impossible choice, the outcome of which he can only regret.

OTTO DE KAT
Translated from the Dutch by Ina Rilke

◆

JULIA

Complete and Unabridged

ULVERSCROFT
Leicester

First published in Great Britain in 2011 by
MacLehose Press
an imprint of
Quercus
London

First Large Print Edition
published 2014
by arrangement with
Quercus
London

The moral right of the author has been asserted

A catalogue record for this book is available
from the British Library.

ISBN 978-1-4448-2001-0

Published by
F. A. Thorpe (Publishing)
Anstey, Leicestershire

Set by Words & Graphics Ltd.
Anstey, Leicestershire
Printed and bound in Great Britain by
T. J. International Ltd., Padstow, Cornwall

This book is printed on acid-free paper

For my mother

1

Sunday was his day off, as was Monday. Although free, he was always on call, so he avoided going to the house on those days. This particular Sunday afternoon he dropped by to take a look at the car; the engine had been stalling. Vague suspicion when he did not see Meneer Dudok in his usual place at his desk. Peaceful garden, terrace door half open, the boss's reclining chair with a rumpled rug beside it. The lawn led down to a fen with water lilies. Dragonflies whirred above the surface. Nothing untoward, a hot Sunday in August, just the warning bell of a railway crossing and the slur of car tyres on the asphalt beyond.

He walked around De Venhorst, as the house was inevitably named after the fen, to the back, glancing up at the balcony in case Dudok was there, before going into the garage to check the old, dark-green Wolseley. He raised the bonnet without thinking, then hesitated. Something was not quite right, he could sense it. He had better go and tell Meneer Dudok he had arrived. Ignoring the terrace, he took his key and let himself in by the front door.

1

Not a sound. He listened out for the voice to boom from upstairs: 'Van Dijk, is that you?' Nothing.

At first sight the kitchen looked the same as he had left it, everything tidied away, dishwasher empty and ajar. But a cupboard door was open. A saucepan on the hob, he noted, a couple of spoons on the draining-board. He knew Dudok seldom went into the kitchen: 'Your department, Van Dijk.' The previous day he had left his boss's lunch consisting of two cheese sandwiches under a glass cover on the dining-room table with a thermos of tea beside it.

'Meneer Dudok,' he called out warily.

'Meneer Dudok,' louder this time. He felt another twinge of misgiving, stronger than before. A threat he had felt for years, a niggling fear. Christaan Dudok, the gentleman who employed Van Dijk as driver, butler and general factotum, Christiaan Dudok, aged seventy-two, was not answering.

He found him upstairs in the study, a few paces from his desk. His hand across the threshold, the door half open. White and cold, in the middle of summer.

Van Dijk grunted. He felt for a pulse in the neck, then spotted a cereal bowl standing on the desk with a silver spoon beside it. A box of tablets, nondescript, unfamiliar label.

Suicide for the posh. That's what it was, no doubt about it: his Meneer Dudok had taken his own life. The evidence was all there. Oatmeal porridge. He had read somewhere that crushing the tablets into porridge made them easier to swallow. The immaculate dark suit from Spalton and Maas, lowest button of the waistcoat undone, fob watch in place — it was obvious at a glance that this was a man of standing, a man whom death had not taken unawares. The black, well-polished toecaps glinted in the shaft of sunlight slanting across his legs.

Van Dijk began to tremble, partly out of shock, but mainly out of indignation. There lay his boss, confound him, the fastidious, ever-reserved Meneer Dudok, sprawled in a pose that was positively inviting by his standards. The arms spread, one leg flexed beneath the other, the hands open, the head tilted sideways.

This was anything but his department.

He reached the telephone in three strides, dialled his boss's doctor. He counted the times the phone rang as he cast his eye over the desk, which was not as orderly as usual. Dudok had been reading, looking things up, presumably. He spoke briefly to the doctor, who said he would come round at once. The books had been hurriedly laid on the table,

3

some open at pages with notes scribbled in the margin. And an old, yellowed newspaper, too faint to read at first glance. That was where Dudok must have been sitting as he ate his porridge. Was there a farewell note? He hunted around, found nothing, and suddenly felt ashamed of his inquisitiveness. Had he got it all wrong? Could it not just have been heart failure? He crouched down beside Dudok, felt an urge to straighten the jacket and make perfect the tie, which was slightly askew. Wearing a tie on a hot summer's day, how chic was that. Only once had he caught his boss wearing a shirt with short sleeves and no tie — that was as far as his casual mode had ever gone. But then the weather had been tropical — 'uncivilized', in Meneer Dudok's parlance.

No, not the heart, this was deliberate. His health had been fine, well, except that he had gone off his head, obviously. Van Dijk tried not to give in to the anger rising in him, anger at his boss for leaving him in the lurch, not a word of warning, let alone of thanks. Dying like this, it wasn't good form. Not what one would expect of a gentleman like Dudok, but what did he know, perhaps it was a very brave and dignified thing to do in his case. Van Dijk would not dream of doing it himself.

It seemed an eternity before the doctor

arrived. Van Dijk felt uneasy being with Dudok, and began to wander around, in and out of the study, stepping over the one stretched leg each time. He even sat down for a moment at the desk, on the spindly chair with the fine cane-work back and slender armrests. It was a tight squeeze, a seat made for city folk with neither brawn nor paunch. Books as far as the eye could see in this room, piled up on side tables, lining the walls around the large window, crammed into an antique revolving bookcase in the corner, enough to drive anyone mad. A mass of grey, brown, burgundy, dark-green bindings, classical lettering on the spines. Ter Braak, he read slowly, Vestdijk, Du Perron, Nijhoff, Marsman — a whole graveyard of names he had never heard of. He lifted the yellowed newspaper, which was on the verge of falling apart. It was printed in an unfamiliar font. He made out the title with some difficulty: *Lübecker Generalanzeiger*, and the date: *2 April, 1942*. A list of names on the front page had been ringed in ink.

Van Dijk heard the doctor coming up the stairs; apparently he had forgotten to shut the front door. He quickly put down the newspaper, coughed, and uttered a greeting.

'I spoke to him only last night, Doctor. At around midnight, when I dropped him off near the railway crossing down the road, and I found him here today at four. The clock in the hall downstairs was just striking, that's how I know exactly what time it was.'

The doctor moved at a snail's pace, the normal speed for this neck of the woods. And quite right too, thought Van Dijk, no point in rushing about in this heat. The verdict came as no surprise: death by his own hand.

'Painless.'

Still, there must have been a fair amount of pain before getting this far. His employer, with his half-melancholic, half-sarcastic gaze, was not a man of impulse. This must have taken some time in the planning.

'Look, Vesparax tablets. Saved them up over a couple of months at least, I would say. From Belgium, because they are illegal here. He must have known their strength, and how many to take. Professional job,' the doctor observed dryly.

Van Dijk was baffled. Why had Meneer Dudok never breathed a word during all those long car journeys to the factory and back? Thousands of kilometres of keeping mum, and all that misery immediately beneath the surface. Dudok, diagonally behind him on the back seat, forever with his newspaper, reading light on, cigarette at the ready. If you added it all up they had spent

6

whole months on the road, day and night in their motorized den. But no talking, oh no, nothing personal ever, not the slightest hint of what must have been spinning round in his brain, constricting his windpipe, eating away at him.

'This will do, Van Dijk, you can drop me off here. I feel like walking the rest of the way.'

That was yesterday evening. He had been astonished, as his boss was never one to walk; in fact he insisted on being driven everywhere — right into his study, had that been possible. Walking was beneath him. The last stretch in the dark, the sandy path along the maize fields. Taking a sharp bend as he drove off, he had glimpsed Meneer Dudok standing with his head thrown back gazing at the sky, which was almost white with stars. He was barely distinguishable from the maize; there was not a breath of wind, nothing stirred.

He had parked the car in the garage and gone home. He had been told not to wait. When Meneer Dudok climbed out of the car he had patted him briefly on the shoulder — something he never did. He never touched anyone if he could avoid it.

'The weather is still very pleasant. Good night, Van Dijk.'

Just as he was shutting the car door he

noticed the diary lying on the back seat.

'Your diary, sir.'

'That's all right, I shan't be needing it. Later will do.'

So the diary must still be in the car, he thought, and excused himself. In the garage he lowered the bonnet of the car and peered through the rear window. The diary was there. He slipped it into his pocket, meaning to look at it when the doctor was gone. This time he came into the house via the terrace. Sitting room, easy chairs, pictures, grand piano, lampshades: to him the whole place was already shrouded in dust covers, swaddled, unearthly quiet, frozen. Ready for sale and removal. He picked his way across, feeling ungainly among the assembled heirlooms. He could hear the doctor on the telephone upstairs. Calm voice, measured, as if he were listening even as he spoke. He made several calls in succession. Who was he was telephoning, and wasn't it about time they notified the next of kin?

'The police will arrive shortly. Would you stay here? I have a house call to make.'

Of course he would stay. He asked if he should try to get in touch with Meneer Dudok's brother and sister. Not just yet, wait until the police have been.

The doctor departed, wheels crunching

over the gravel. Van Dijk watched the car go as he wandered over to the water's edge. A narrow strip of grass bordered the small lake. Unsettled and disoriented, he sent some pebbles skimming across the surface, counting the times they bounced. On an impulse he took a handful of gravel and hurled it into the lake. Meneer Dudok had pulled a fast one, leaving him stuck with some other job to find. He had done everything for the old man, taken his clothes to the drycleaner's, cooked for him, driven him all over the country, put up with his foibles and silences, helped him get over the death of his wife. How long was it since she had passed away? Seven years now, seven years of being his boss's shadow, his stick to lean on, his pillar of support. Fetching medicines, chopping firewood, repairing everything under the sun. That it should come to this: a boss who crushed death pills into his porridge and then gobbled it up. Distasteful, selfish, pointless. Saving all that junk on the sly, knowing exactly how much he would need. His silhouette against the maize field. How odd it had seemed, Dudok wanting to be dropped off there. Now he could see why: his last stroll, his last starry sky, perhaps even a last attempt to breathe freely. A solitary figure staring into space, raising his eyes to the filaments of the

9

Milky Way in a universe beyond comprehension. Would he have heard the distant hum of the tractor bringing in the hay until late into the night?

Van Dijk clenched his fist, screwed up his eyes against the tears, then let go. He wept. That was not like him, and soon he stopped. He felt slightly better, began to put some order into his thoughts. The diary — there was bound to be something in there. He took out the familiar dark leather-bound booklet. Ribbon marker on the Saturday; used until the last, evidently. The Sunday was blank. Appointments for next week, a shareholders' meeting, dinner with Jenny, lunch in Rotterdam. No trace of any preparations, no hint of anything out of the ordinary. September: dentist, bank manager, two birthdays. October: three trips to the west of the country. November, just one entry, on the 9th, where it said in Dudok's clear hand: The Night, with two capital letters. Van Dijk riffled through the pages: blank for the rest of the year.

A pair of moorhens shot away over the lake, their feet scooping the water. Their amazing, nervous speed and that illusion of weightlessness always took him by surprise.

The oppressive heat drove him indoors, where he had no desire to be. The chair in front of the long table with bulbous legs by the big window — that was where Meneer Dudok always sat, unless he was upstairs in the study, studying, or doing whatever it was he did there. A flat dish doing service as ashtray, the *Spectator* beside it, a photograph of his late wife on the windowsill, another of 'Stoetie', his friend Edmond van Stoetwegen, and a third of his sister, such was the décor of his final years. Year in year out, whatever the season, he would settle himself by the window as soon as he got home. Imagine having a view like that and seeing nothing.

Van Dijk had a momentary compulsion to sit in Dudok's chair, but checked himself. Suddenly he felt abashed; it would be a lack of respect for the dead man upstairs. He had never sat there before, why do so now? He could sense Dudok all around him. The presence of a corpse immediately affects the atmosphere of a house, so they say, regardless of which room the deceased is kept in, so the stillness becomes eerie and disquieting.

Van Dijk hurried up the stairs, stepped over Dudok once more on his way to the desk. He picked up the newspaper again, peered at the German hieroglyphs. *Lübecker Generalanzeiger, 2 April, 1942.* What was it doing there, why had those names been ringed? They meant nothing to him. He started up from the newspaper; the doorbell was ringing. From the study window he saw two men, one wearing a hat, the other with a briefcase under his arm. Surely not Jehovah's Witnesses, not today of all days. He opened the front door, ready to send them away.

'Police,' the man in the hat said.

2

Emil Jannings loomed life-size from the cinema billboard: *Der Herrscher*, best film at the Venice festival. Nasty-looking piece of work, thought Chris as he cycled along the Mühlen Strasse on his way to the office. He went past several other cinemas and theatres. Downtown Lübeck in the morning was all bicycles and pedestrians, trams and buses. The streets seethed with work ethic, a prodigious eagerness to be on time. Trade and industry were said to be booming, and it was true.

February 1938. The morning turned out surprisingly mild and sunny, with the scent of spring in the air. Chris Dudok was lodged in an historic building on the Musterbahn. Everything about Lübeck was historic. Hatless and scarfless, with his overcoat unbuttoned, he pedalled to Lubecawerke, a modern plant manufacturing cooling installations and milk powder machines. His father owned a similar factory in Holland, but that had not stopped them from taking him on, possibly with a view to gaining inside information about the rival Dutch company.

He was to succeed his father the following year. It did not bear thinking about. He would rather have Ter Braak or Van Schendel to pore over than the turgid prose of his father's business reports. The idea of having to exchange Nietzsche for the financial pages made him choke. He was choking anyway. The spirit of the times seized him by the throat. Crazed masses rallied on a whim, marching and parading with soldierly discipline, Lübeck thrumming with excitement for the leader's new teachings. There was no getting away from the man. He appeared not to be taken so seriously in Holland, as though his ravings were put through a strain at the border. But the artist from Vienna was crafty, in his opinion, barking mad, but very clever. The radio seemed invented expressly for him, forever blasting into people's sitting rooms. Nobody thought to switch him off.

'The engineers here work twelve hours a day,' he reported to his parents, meaning that he feared there would not be much opportunity for reading. He was hard put to focus on the latest trends in wage systems, dictaphones, adding machines, all of them aimed at streamlining production, raising output.

At first he daydreamed of escape. He dearly wanted to forget the factory. His father, suddenly taken ill, had announced his intention to hand over the reins. To him, Chris. Good grief — having to run a machine factory, a family business, with a brother, a sister and a father hovering in the background.

But during these last days and weeks his mood had changed; thoughts of his father's factory had waned, the panic subsided. Cycling to Lubecawerke ceased to be a duty, it was something to look forward to. Nonetheless, he pedalled at his leisure, even freewheeling now and then. As though he needed to take his time preparing himself for her, picturing her, almost dreading having to face up to her and match her speed, terrified of disappointing her. Julia.

February in Lübeck, a town like an oyster. Hard to prise open, but once inside she enfolded you, elderly as she was, and not quite herself of late. Chris lived in the basement of a pale-yellow building on the fringe of the Altstadt. He had a view of the street and the constant passing of legs. A glance out of the window was enough to register the state of the country. The alacrity, the firm steps, the brisk gait. His daily dose of optimism administered upon waking. Gratis.

Grist to the mill for Leni Riefenstahl, the film-maker. Legs for the Reich, feet on their

15

way to work, people striding ahead with blind faith in better days. Pavement, sunshine, camera roll! Chris went to the cinema as often as he could, or to the theatre. Everyone was doing the same, the queues were endless. Numbness, escape, flight from the fierce pace of progress. Cod psychology alright, but in his case it was valid. Numbness was what he was after; for him the evenings meant hours of sharpened insight, of anxiety as to whether he stood the slightest chance with Julia.

Down the Breite Strasse he went, then the Burg Strasse, under the arches of the Burgtor, across the bridge and into open countryside. The scent of forest and manure. Age-old, neglected feelings. Onward to Julia, as if he were after something that had been inexplicably taken from him as a child. What exactly it was that had been stolen he did not know. All he knew was the void left in its wake.

Lubecawerke became synonymous with Julia. Entering the long corridor with the drawing section at the end gave him a sense of lightness. More than that, of fulfilment. As though he were catching up on his life, regaining his balance, with the ground growing firm under his step. It had been going on for weeks.

He had only seen her from afar, around the engineer's wing. He had not met her, let

16

alone talked to her.

Chris occupied a small office adjoining that of the managing director, Herr Knollenberg, who sent for him each morning to enquire how things stood, to bring him up to date on company news, and wish him a productive day.

It was during one of those brief visits to the executive office that she had come in with a query. Knollenberg introduced them and proceeded to turn his full attention to her. Chris had time to observe her closely. Never had he encountered a woman like her. Composed, liberated, resolute. His imagination ran wild: dance with me, come to the theatre with me, fall into my arms, touch me, tell me who you are. What? This is quite out of character, Chris. Get a grip.

In the days that followed he made every effort to cross paths with her. He even managed to talk to her now and then. His foreign accent, his somewhat gauche politeness and his shy admiration were not lost on her, so much was clear. They talked about faraway people, faraway places, about the past. Now and then they touched on what the newspapers were saying and failing to say, once in a while on the radio man. But always lightly, casually, like people on a pleasure boat. Chris looked at her, she saw him looking. They talked, joked, riposted, kept

17

thinking up nice things to say to each other. Their eyes met. Chris held open doors for her, she went through them.

Was the frequency of her visits to the company director a coincidence? One day, on leaving Knollenberg's office, she put her head round the door of his room.

'Don't work too hard, now. No need for them to know all our secrets over in Holland.' She laughed.

'As long as I haven't deciphered you I shall stay right here, nose to the grindstone.'

She laughed again. 'Not an easy code to crack, Chris. Keep trying.'

Playful digs, snatches of songs, small delights. Lubecawerke, the blandest, most featureless place imaginable. But behind the façade of machinery and drawing boards there was Julia. Julia Bender, engineer.

The letters he received from his father, and particularly from his Dutch girlfriend, became more urgent and demanding by the day, but he put them aside. Spring, going on summer, Lübeck and Julia, why worry about mundane things like the family business or settling down.

If only he could be light-footed like Julia, a free spirit like her, untrammelled by duty or authority. He had no wish to contemplate the gravity of the political situation. Who was she, where did that outrageous breeziness come from, that infectious, wilful independence? Free of all convention, and yet able to live up to the expectations of Lubecawerke's management.

A few weeks went by before he plucked up courage: might he invite her to dinner, or to the cinema, or perhaps to a café?

'Grand-Café Elzas, on the corner between the Breite Strasse and the Hüx Strasse. Tomorrow at six?'

He nodded, speechless. Not for one moment had he dared to suppose she would say yes.

'Anything wrong with Grand-Café Elzas, Chris? You've gone all quiet.' Then, archly: 'I'll wear a rose on my hat, so you'll know which one is me.'

'Oh, I'd pick you out among thousands, Julia, but a hat with roses, now that I do like, so yes, please.'

Ping-pong ball from her side, badminton shuttle from his. Fast versus slow, both to good effect. He countered her speed with his bashful concentration, tried to keep pace with her in his own way, lurching a little as he fell headlong in love. In love, what an expression, what a prosaic way of expressing what he felt in her presence. The void ceased to exist the moment he saw her, his revulsion at what was going on around him waned, as did his gloom about his own prospects, his dread of living a life that was not of his own choosing. All these things left him as long as he was with her. Did that mean he had fallen in love? So be it, then, he was in love. But was that not dangerously close to love per se, the unattainable, dreamed-of, redoubtable state of loving?

The stuff of novels, romantic imaginings, so he had convinced himself early on. He had immersed himself in philosophy, in Schopenhauer and Nietzsche, the misogynists, the deniers of love. They had deposited layer upon layer of their pessimism in his brain, rather to his own satisfaction. Love, ha! How could he ever fall prey to romance and sentimentality? Love existed solely in the minds of the needy and the weak.

And now? Going home meant pressure to get married and perhaps, worse still, becoming a father. Running a factory, listening to complaints, making money, telling other people what to do. He could not do any of those things, not any more. He would resist; he would not return.

Julia dominated his brain, seeped into the divisions and seams of his soul — a soul he no longer believed in — arousing in him the kind of emotion his philosophers despised. Julia. It was getting worse by the day. He said nothing, afraid to put her off.

Grand-Café Elzas was decked with Austrian and German flags, and in festive mood when Chris entered at six o'clock. Lübeck in March was cold, the Baltic was round the corner, it was snowing. From his table by the tall window he had a view of the entrance and the street outside. The massive revolving door, mahogany with brass handrails, created regular draughts. The place filled up rapidly, and he had to defend the vacant chair opposite him several times. Austrian flags: the Germans had 'come to Austria's aid', their beneficent tanks had rolled across the border, where all was in perfect readiness: the doses of deceit and betrayal had never been heavier. The day after the invasion there was a map of Greater Germany on display in every shop window. Austria was no more, it was a flag without a nation, a puff of wind in the storm of the Reich.

He scanned the faces of the crowd. Was the mood really as festive as he had surmised on arrival? He was not sure. There was a forced note in the waiter's jollity; the dull look in his eyes seemed at odds with the triumphant headline of his newspaper: 'Germany rejoices in welcoming a lost people!'

Chris quickly laid the paper aside. Germany was adrift, a festering mess, the whole country in the grip of terror. He registered this, kept abreast of the news, and increasingly felt himself an outsider, a powerless foreigner. He cycled to work in the morning and back at night filled with affection for the old Hanseatic town, and fearful of what lay in store. Outside the office people kept out of his way, politely but unmistakably. As though the ranks had to remain serried, as though the young Dutchman were an intrusion on their thoughts. That was to be avoided. Thinking was a strictly private affair, off limits.

'Thinking's not something we do anymore,' Julia had said. Laughing, always laughing, against the stream.

The revolving door turned for the umpteenth time. Julia. He let her look around, did not leap to his feet to attract her attention. He had lived towards this, afraid until the last that she would not turn up, afraid that she would have to do overtime at the factory, afraid of everything. He could not get enough of seeing her actually standing there, knowing that she was looking out for him, that she wanted to find him. How had that miracle happened? She spotted him sooner than he had hoped. In a few strides she was at his table, and before he had time to stand up, she said: 'The roses were sold out, no wonder you didn't recognize me.'

22

'Couldn't you have got some fake Edelweiss instead?'

Julia's expression changed, her gaiety gone at a stroke.

'Bastards. Bastards, every one of them,' she said, tapping the folded newspaper lying on the table between them.

'Don't believe them, Chris. It's all lies. Every newspaper, every poster, every letter in this country is censored, controlled, dictated.'

She had spoken in an undertone, he noted, but he did not think anybody could have overheard her in the hubbub of voices. You would need a megaphone to talk to the people at the next table.

Censored, controlled, dictated, the words went round and round in his head long after they had left the café.

Over the weeks since they first met there had been a gradual rapprochement between them, gentle, tentative, even cautious. And so the days at Lubecawerke had passed, with Chris in mounting excitement as to whether Julia would deign to show herself. He kept slipping out into the corridor past Knollenberg's office towards the technical drawing section, a random stack of papers under his arm, a folder to deliver nowhere. He walked with an air of purpose, absorbed in his self-imposed assignment, glancing into the room she shared with another engineer. He often saw her by the window overlooking the courtyard, with her back to him, her hands on her drawing board. What was she designing, what was she thinking, how could she concentrate on her work, did she not know how he felt?

'What will you have to drink?' The waiter appeared before Chris had time to call him. With a smile that utterly belied her earlier imprecations against the powers-that-be, Julia ordered a glass of white wine. Chris followed suit. They kept silent a moment, listening to the clamour, a sea of voices. Her outburst still hung in the air, her vehemence, her scathing indictment of the regime. She obviously trusted him, or she would never have spoken in that way.

'And what do you think of our Knollenberg?' she asked abruptly.

'I imagine he believes what the papers say.'

'He has relatives in Austria. I bet he's thrilled.' Sarcasm, with a tinge of sadness.

Chris longed to take her in his arms, to sweep off her hat in full view of everyone, loosen her hair, kiss her eyes. Of course he did no such thing. Out of the question that he should move closer to her, be it merely an arm's length between them, or the news-paper, or the café table, or a folder of

24

documents, or Knollenberg.

He raised his glass, clinked with hers, in what he imagined a bold move of camaraderie. She looked at him as she drank. Quietly, sweetly, a momentary flicker of uncertainty in her eyes. He did not dare to ask any questions, for all that he longed to know where she came from, where she lived, what she did with her time, what her childhood had been like. He was bursting with questions, had been framing them in his mind all day so as to be ready for the right moment, which never seemed to arrive.

The musicians at the back played for all they were worth, but they were drowned out by the din of the packed café. This Saturday evening had clearly been billed as a gala event. Ladies in their finery, spruced-up men. But what was intended as a celebration of the Austrian 'homecoming' had not yet caught on. There was a certain grimness to the animation of the crowd, people seemed to be bracing themselves against something — against what, really? Hard times, the onslaught of violence, war? War, the never-mentioned word that was on everyone's mind.

'If you all carry on like this for much longer there's bound to be a war, Julia.'

'You all?' She stared at him, aghast.

'Who else is there?' the words were out of

his mouth before he knew it.

'Oh, there are lots of others, Chris. All over the place, all over the country. Hundreds and thousands of us. Only, we're all stuck in overcrowded barracks, without permission to leave. Buchenwald, Dachau, Sachsenhausen, the mere mention of those places can get you into trouble.'

'What about you then?'

'I don't belong anywhere; I have no desire to belong. You will never find me in any of those barracks, I would rather die.'

Shocked by her words, Chris had no answer. Just then a small party of brown-shirted *Sturmabteilung* youths made their entrance. Five newcomers in a crowd of over two hundred. Nonetheless, they caused an immediate stir, with the orchestra faltering and conversations subsiding. Julia seized the newspaper and spread it out, pointing to a photograph.

'Carry on talking, Chris, just carry on.'

He saw them approach, trooping across the café in the direction of the music, the tallest in the lead, the less brawny in his wake.

'Don't look, Chris. Ignore them. What were we talking about — oh yes, it was Knollenberg, wasn't it?'

The leader of the pack tapped the conductor on the shoulder and said something to

26

him. The conductor smiled, squared his shoulders and raised his baton for the song. The crowd responded on cue with a rising swell of voices, the last lingering doubts melting away into the resounding chorus. The Horst Wessel song: flag up high, ranks tightly closed, the storm-troopers march with calm, firm steps.

The anthem thundered around them. Chris and Julia did not join in. They waited for it to pass, for the flag to be lowered, the ranks broken up, the glasses replenished.

The crowd sang loud and clear, they knew the words by heart. Bread and freedom, the end of slavery was nigh.

Then off they went again, holsters on hips, menace in five-fold. They knew how the land lay, they were aware of their might. Two hundred people, arms raised in salute, staring after them. It could not be long now.

Julia stood up, ramrod straight, newspaper under her elbow, her gaze fixed on the five rowdies making their way to the revolving door. The brown battalion thudded past the dark windows. It was still snowing.

'Darlings,' murmured Julia. 'Darling boys. Where for the love of God are their mothers?'

Chris laughed. 'Your love knows no bounds, does it?'

'Nor do their jackboots. There's going to be a war, Chris, I know it and so do you. And then what will you do over in Holland?'

'Ask for your extradition, of course.'

She was concerned about him, thought Chris; she cared, she had wanted to see him. Would he dare now, would he dare to take her hand? The waiter appeared, the moment passed. He had not touched her, but perhaps he had reached her.

3

The sandy footpath lay in darkness each way. He continued to hear the car for some time, the soft rumble of the low gear in which Van Dijk drove away. It was hardly any distance from De Venhorst that he had asked to be dropped off. The maize stood tall.

It was a fifteen-minute walk, no more than that. Quarter of an hour across the fields, with the last stretch along some thatched villas, all in the pitch dark. No risk of meeting anyone, it was too late in the day, even for people walking their dogs. Dudok watched as Van Dijk took the bend, the headlights sweeping over the meadow. Gone. The air still thick with heat, a moonless night in August, the occasional bright streak of a falling star. He had no wishes to make, not any more. Or maybe just one: to fall into that gaping universe out there. In a flash. How wonderful simply to fall, to hurtle through space, infinitely alone, ad infinitum. His entire life had been geared to such a fall. He had the feeling there had always been people standing in his way, even as a child. But fall he would, into the unlimited depths of a well, wordless, echoless, heartless. He had everything planned, nothing could go wrong now. Just as well he had no children. No wife either. Died seven years ago. Not of natural causes, he sometimes thought. Death by neglect, by deficiency.

He had loved her, oh yes. Intermittently. Out of decency, out of habit, or just by default?

He looked up at the sky, raised his hat with one hand and patted his hair with the other. Chaos, black holes, randomness. There were no answers to anything, as he had always known. This was hotly disputed by his younger sister, forever doing battle with him about the soul and redemption. Let her talk, let her hope and await, let her believe and pray — nothing could sway him from his stony belief. There was nothing to stop him now from doing what everyone would disapprove of. He would be the one to set in motion his own escape, his fall.

The time had finally come. He looked forward to it, like a child on a beach anticipating high tide. One last fifteen-minute stroll, one last look at the mist rising from the fen by the house. The idea of one last did not bother him, it was a statement of fact. The stopwatch in his head registered the time, counted the minutes, set the hour. He was not one for drama. All over, forgotten, suppressed.

Staring into space, he caught the far-off sound of tractors: farmers bringing in the harvest far into the night. A comforting sound. He listened intently, curiously satisfied with the image it brought to mind: taciturn farmers with horse-drawn carts. Hay stacked thickly all around, fanning out in rising mounds. Men hoisting pitchforks way above their heads, opening great umbrellas of grass. At ten years old, his grandfather's farm near Doesburg had been his castle. All that land, the orchards, the cows and horses, cattle for slaughter, farmhands, a yard full of wagons. Next to no machinery, manual labour was the norm. Power was horse power; supper came from the chopping block next to the chicken run. The farmyard was a maze of opportunity for a city boy of ten: a lost cause, poor lad, in his grandfather's eyes. Even then he was between two worlds, cut off from the old roots, a pale-faced bookworm. Aged ten he sat on a one-legged milking stool with his cheek against the cow's flank and the warmth of the blue-veined udder in his hands. He held the reins of the horse-drawn wagon laden with potatoes, or beets, or chickens in baskets, to sell at the market. A boy among grown men, absorbing their country dialect, savouring the words of an adventurous, enviable way of life.

That was where it had all started, where it first hit him, there on his grandfather's land: he was there and yet he was not. The farm meant being alive, it meant lying sprawled on the hay, hearing the thud of horses' hooves, even a pig being slaughtered in the yard. The land, his land, the sun rising over the cows as he milked them, a calf being born by the light of lanterns. The clang of a milk pail on the cobbles, the scent of apples spread out in the barn.

But he did not belong there. Home was the city, the factory he would inherit one day, the books he read, the stylized life of a child among well-spoken adults. Chris Dudok, future company director, future erudite, future restless soul.

He used to have dreams about being allowed to live with his grandfather forever.

The starry sky was veiled with white. Dudok stared on, unable to tear himself away from the vastness, from the memories swarming at him from all sides. The living body in rebellion against slaughter, the cow on her way to the abattoir, looking round at the meadow and the farmer's hands, the chicken failing to escape the axe, the squealing pig. Back, turn back, take another path through the wood, there are so many ways of coming home. An owl hooted close by, perfecting the stillness.

4

The weeks passed. April arrived with a welter of colours, and a welter of hesitations. Each day Chris cycled from the Musterbahn to Lubecawerke and back, exhilarated, in turmoil. He defied the grimness of the town. Since the Anschluss Lübeck had not become any sunnier. The generals' dance reverberated in the streets and across harbours and wharves, preparations were being made on all fronts.

This April morning was different. Chris set off on his daily ride to the office, sunk in thought. He went past the *Stadstheater*, where the previous evening he had seen a spine-chilling performance. Stage direction and lead role by Andreas Bender. Her surname.

A classic drama, with a main character making an unexpected bid for freedom. He had leapt down from the stage into the auditorium, and had walked straight out of the theatre into the town square. Gone, absorbed into the crowd, into the night. An ideal solution. Not for him though, Chris realized, for all that he recognized the desire.

He had felt it that very morning, that very day.

A whole day spent in the drawing section, engineers hunched over their desks, cigarettes between their lips. He toured all the sections systematically, from warehouse to executive headquarters. People seemed well-disposed towards him, there was no furtiveness, he was given all the information he requested. They knew he was there to learn about the business, espionage obviously did not cross their minds. A young chap from Holland, nothing special, reliable, even-tempered.

Yet his temper was anything but even. His father's illness had taken him by surprise, and the prospect of going back frequently caused him to panic. The parleying had already begun. In the past week there had been further letters from his father, brimming with advice, instructions and admonishments. He could barely bring himself to read them, the mere mention of 'the factory' being both distasteful and frustrating to him. The factory: stamping ground of his boyhood.

It had been there for as long as he could remember, the nondescript grey building along the canal, with a door set into a much larger door giving access to the workplace. It was like stepping into a wild west. Men in enormous goggles wielding elongated pistols which spat fire. Silvery metal shavings in curly heaps, the clank and rattle of winches and cranes. Huge rollers on gantries, men shouting, a sickly smell of oil, a fairground ghost-house, deafening crashes running the length of the great hall. The warehouseman used to take him by the hand and lead him safely across. Thick, calloused fingers — how was he supposed to provide leadership for men like that? Where would he lead them to, and how?

True, he had a degree in economics, but how relevant was that in the cut and thrust of everyday life? Economics was the terrain of hope, hope for more and better and longer. Emperor's new clothes embroidered with fancy numbers and percentages. Economists were confabulators, priests to a congregation of shortsighted believers who were convinced of their perfect vision. Their science was nothing but an imaginary bridge spanning an abyss. He was sick and tired of the high-flown rhetoric. In the end every man had to decide for himself. There was no formula or recipe for running an enterprise with success, although you wouldn't have thought so here in Lübeck, and all over Germany too, for that matter. The zeal, the frenzy, the all-consuming will to grow and succeed took his breath away.

Lubecawerke was but a pinhead on the map of growth. Yet in each division of the plant he was made to feel that it was there, before his very eyes, that the country's future was being constructed. Each act served the same end, each day brought them closer to their goal. He was amazed by the speed and efficiency, the dogged commitment, the common desire. The radio man was in their heads. If he swerved they swerved, if he halted so too did they, if he called they came running.

Chris cycled on. The night at the theatre clung to him, a night unlike any other, the onset of a tragedy, the first domino to fall. Just before the curtain went up there had been a sudden hush. Doors that were already closed flew open, spotlights were beamed on the front row, bathing it in a red glare. And there they were, a small party of men with a black-suited figure in the middle. The audience rose as one, raised their arms and shouted the name of the radio man, the painter of churches, flowers and landscapes. His deputy turned slowly to face them, raised a limp hand and tapped his aide on the shoulder with his glove. Chris sat alone in a cage of arms, imprisoned in a steel salute. Men and women, everyone standing, everyone calling out in unison, their faces shining with reverence for the magician in their lives.

For a moment he was overcome; the veneration was almost tangible. The arrival of a stand-in for the leader was enough to galvanize an entire auditorium. Theatre, what else?

A play culminating in the lead actor leaping down from the stage, and proceeding to stare, pale and perspiring, still in the transports of his role, at the black-suited man in the front row. For an instant he even seemed about to give the people's salute, but no. He raised his eyes, smiled, and then, caught in the spotlight, strode towards the exit. The audience sat in bewildered, breathless silence, presided over by the slighted, grim-faced, flunkey of the Most High. Hardly anyone noticed the man from his entourage going in pursuit of the absconding actor just before the lights came on again. But Chris did notice. He understood. There had been no mistaking the actor's expression of scorn and contempt. It had been a provocation, a subversive act, a public indictment.

Cycling past the city theatre on the Beckergrube, near the Breite Strasse, he noted its closed-down look. 'Tonight's performance cancelled' it said on a large sheet of plain paper beside the entrance. He was not surprised by the announcement, just by its early appearance.

But the night at the theatre had been momentous for another reason, too.

Julia had been sitting two rows ahead of him. Suddenly she was there, out of the blue, a sign from a world of angels, a quiet bird winging over a field before nightfall. The sight of her there in her theatre seat would stay with him forever, like everything else about her.

As far as he could tell she was the only other person in the audience to remain seated when black-suit and his gang made their appearance. She had arrived at the last minute; the house lights had already dimmed. He could see she was out of breath. She must have come running, he reckoned, that would be just like her. She was diagonally in front of him, and he craned his neck to catch a glimpse of her face. He saw how she froze when everyone stood up, how the colour drained from her cheeks, how she kept perfectly still. When everyone sat down again she seemed to breathe a sigh of relief. She looked round furtively, and spotted him. Chris nodded, she nodded back, her eyes holding his for seconds on end. She had been quicker than him to leave after the performance. She already had her coat on and was heading for the exit while he was queuing at the cloakroom. He cursed his own slowness, his coat was taking an eternity, and she was out of the theatre before he could do anything about it. He had called her name, people had stared, even recoiled. Had they recognized him as the man who had neglected to give the salute? How little it took to become a pariah, he thought.

Chris kept being overtaken by other bicycles. The city theatre was some way behind him when a car pulled up in front of him, forcing him onto the verge. Two men climbed out with much ado, one of whom addressed him. Papers please. He had his passport on him and handed it over. They inspected it minutely, turning the pages back and forth, their eyes flitting from the photograph to him and back again. Where was he going? Lubecawerke? Did he know a certain Julia Bender? No he did not, the name did not ring a bell and could he go now. Hollander, eh, good country, they would be going there themselves some day, for sure. And they climbed back into their battered Volkswagen, two miserable snitches, misguided patriots, spooks in human guise.

Chris was shaken. Julia Bender, why would they be interested in her, how did they know her name?

He set off again, speeding up now. Normally it was another twenty minutes to the factory, this time it was ten. His eyes stung in the wind, his ears rang with the question: did he know Julia Bender.

No sooner had he entered his office than he was sent for by Knollenberg. On his desk lay a sheet of paper, which he stabbed at with his finger.

'This is from the police. They were here earlier this morning,' he said. 'An act of provocation at the city theatre. You were present, I am told. Was it really that bad?'

Chris said no, nothing had happened. Perhaps that very 'nothing' had caused the problem. Perhaps the people in the front row had been offended by the way the actor had stood there looking at them, saying not a word, after which he had smiled and made off. Chris explained what the play was about, succinctly, hurriedly, impatient to run to the drawing section and warn Julia. Her section was situated at the other end of the executive wing, the nerve centre of the enterprise. That was where the future was being constructed, where machines were conceived which would not materialize until two, three years hence.

'Did you notice anything else? I gather you remained seated during the salute to our leadership?' Two questions to which no reply was expected. Knollenberg was well informed; Chris could only stare in wonderment.

'Do you know Julia Bender?' The same question again.

'Of course I do, Herr Knollenberg. She works here, about twenty metres away from your office in fact. You introduced me to her yourself.'

Knollenberg nodded. 'I told them you were probably not acquainted with her. She did not come to work this morning, by the way. Would you be so kind as to go to her house and deliver this note to her? If she is out, which I expect to be the case, you can drop it in her letter box.' Chris took the envelope.

'Right away, Herr Knollenberg?'

Yes, gestured his boss. 'A letter of dismissal, I am sorry to say.' Knollenberg seemed ill at ease. He crossed to the window, drummed his fingers on the central heating. 'Most unfortunate,' was all he was heard to mumble.

Chris turned and left slowly, past the secretary's office and his own, and went on his way. As quickly as he had pedalled to Lubecawerke that morning, so slowly and diffidently did he proceed on his return journey, clutching the envelope, his coat strapped to the carrier, the spring sunshine on his back. She lived along from the theatre on the Glockengiesser Strasse, with trees on either side. Number 27 had no fewer than eight apartments. A plate fixed to the wall bearing a list of names and bells, no sign of a letter box. He heard the doorbell ring directly above him, a hollow, desolate sound. Nothing stirred.

He rang several times, took a step back, saw no-one. He pushed the envelope under the door, heard it sliding over the floorboards.

The traffic thickened. He turned into the Breite Strasse, wheeling his bike, for he could not bring himself to ride it. The street was alive with the kind of bustle that can be wondrously soothing, just by absorbing you into an impersonal and therefore reassuring communality. Comforting, too, without the need for a pat on the shoulder or a clasped hand; a clear, entirely impartial stream into which your life is subsumed like a thing, a piece of wood cast in a river. You drift along. Chris wished for nothing more. He stopped at the first café terrace that was open. The sounds from the square beyond and the voices of early customers ordering coffee reached him faintly as he sat on his cane chair, dazed by his mission, by the sheer pace of events. And overcome when he was joined at his table by a woman who removed her sunglasses and said 'Hello, Chris.'

Julia Bender.

'Julia.' He glanced around furtively. 'Julia, they're looking for you, what are you doing here?'

She gave a short laugh. 'I know, let them look. I saw you delivering a letter. My dismissal, I suppose?'

'How on earth did you know?'

'It's happened before. My previous boss came to deliver it in person, but thank goodness Knollenberg sent you. I was just coming down the street, trying to make up my mind whether to go home or not. Now at least I can have a word with you.'

Chris said nothing. He could hear his own silence as he tried to start a sentence. She smiled, she was ahead of the game, she put her hand on his sleeve.

'Just being a foreigner makes you suspect in this country. Do you think you're being followed?'

He told her about being stopped that morning, and being asked whether he knew her.

'And although I am really glad to know you, I denied it flatly. I hope you won't hold that against me. It wasn't cowardice, it was just that I had the impression it was better not to have any idea who you were.'

'Quite right, better not.'

'Don't you think someone might spot us here?'

'No, I doubt you're being followed, there aren't any of those guys about. And they're

43

quite blatant about what they do, you know, you can tell them a mile off. So we're as safe as houses.'

Her relaxed tone calmed him. And attracted him. Everything about her attracted him. This was the second time he had been alone with her outside the office. Their evening in the Café Elzas a few weeks back had left him ablaze. Feelings smouldering inside him had burst into flame. He had walked Julia home. The dusting of snow on her shoulders, their leisurely stroll down the snowy Breite Strasse, where their voices sounded muffled — there were no words to express what he felt. In the distant reaches of his mind he saw himself sitting by a cow again, milk foaming in the pail, hay-shed in the dusk, images of an unconscionable past.

What sort of person was she, what did she do, why had she lost her job? How could she be so relaxed, so smiling? One look and she had the waiter at her side, ordering two coffees before Chris had time to say anything. He kept falling behind, while she steamed effortlessly ahead.

'What an incredible performance it was last night, Julia. That actor, Andreas Bender, is he a relation of yours?'

'My brother. I adore him, he's a huge example to me.'

Julia told him about Andreas. She told him because he asked, and he kept asking just to hear her tell. Snippets of life in an unconventional family, glimpses of an artistic household in Lübeck. Actor father, actress mother, both having trained in Berlin before returning to their native city. Andreas and she grew up thinking the world was all red plush and stage-curtains opening and closing. An irregular existence, with parents who were always out in the evening, or away for weeks on tour, or hanging around for months waiting for new roles.

'My mother used to learn her parts in the kitchen; a whole range of them, from classical repertoire to modern plays. She'd cry and whisper and sing as she stirred the pots and pans on the stove. When I was old enough I took over the cooking, and she'd sit at the kitchen table rehearsing while I made the food. I was her prompter, with cookery book and script side by side in front of me on the draining board. I still tend to have some book lying next to the spinach when I cook. And I listen for my mother's step. She's dead, both my parents are. A car crash somewhere around Munich, after a performance. It was a stupid accident, my father fell asleep at the wheel, apparently, and the car crashed into a tree. They died instantly.'

Chris listened as if his life depended on it. Andreas had followed in his parents' footsteps. As a boy he used to learn his father's roles and act out entire plays for Julia's benefit when they were alone in the evenings. They built a stage in the dining room with crates and planks. Andreas took the lead; his sister's role was to listen to his monologues, and to pat his hand, stroke his face, or throw her arms about him. He danced with her, laughed and cried with her.

'Lights down, Julia! Lights up! Curtain! Applause, Julia, applause!'

Those evenings had been thrilling, they had been completely carried away, just went on and on play-acting. Andr eas told her that he had never acted with more conviction than back home in the dining room. Sixteen or seventeen they had been, children no longer, but in no hurry to grow up. It was a time of incredible freedom of expression, they could be anyone they liked, no holds barred, no audience, just the pair of them united in an unbreakable bond. Outside was obscurity, outside was the *Krach*, the great tragedy about to begin.

'You ought to come with me, Julia, Andreas said one day. Pack your bag, we don't belong here, not in this country, this town, this street. My dear Andreas, I said, much as I'd like to, I want to stand on my own two feet. I want to be an engineer, and I'm going to study in Berlin. Then he said he'd come with me instead, he'd enrol at the drama academy there, see which one of us qualified first.'

Julia eyed Chris, coffee cup in hand: 'He beat me to it. He always won, whatever the competition was about. But I wasn't far behind, a couple more months and I too had my degree.'

While she said this he saw her eyes darting about. She appeared to be relaxed, but she was not. She was taking a risk, and she knew it.

'Andreas has been detained. They want to question me, but I have no intention of giving myself up, obviously. Andreas wouldn't want me to, I am absolutely certain of that. They'll probably put him in a labour camp along with all the other undesirables. What he did last night is dangerous in their eyes, however bizarre and small-minded it may seem to you. Defying their authority, an impertinent look, they'll arrest you for anything. We're among the barbarians here.'

Feeling that he should say something, Chris tried to begin a sentence and then straightaway desisted. Who was he to give warnings and plead with her to be careful? — she was so overwhelmingly in charge. With her professional sharpness she oversaw the situation with a clarity he could not hope to match. What could he do? Where would she go?

'But, Julia, where will you go? You could come with me, of course; I could make arrangements. Shall I?'

He made the offer without thinking, the words were out of his mouth before he knew it. He looked away, spooned some extra sugar into his coffee, stirred at length. Her reply was just that bit slower in coming, that bit more timid and surprised than was her nature.

'Yes, Chris, I shall have to go somewhere, and no, there's no need. Well, on second thoughts, yes, please. I promise I'll leave as soon as possible, and I won't be any trouble. Are you sure you have enough room to spare?'

He nodded carefully, yes he had room. He would make room.

They lapsed into silence. The rumble of traffic seemed to increase, and although their terrace was an interlude in the stream of pedestrians, the noise from the street did not abate.

Chris heard Julia say that she would drop by that evening at eight; it would be dark by then. He explained where he lived. She stood

48

up, shook his hand, picked her way across the terrace and vanished into the milling crowd. She had left money for her coffee on the table. Chris placed his money beside hers; she had been too quick for him, yet again. Of course he had wanted to pay for both of them. Was this a warning that she would keep her distance? A little joke? A signal to be less slow in future? That much, for sure: next to her he felt himself a yokel from Holland.

He had little memory of how he got through the rest of that day. He had returned to the office to find the atmosphere changed, and had busied himself with his vague assignments in a suddenly hostile environment. Knollenberg enquired whether he had managed to deliver the letter. Embarrassment and remorse were written all over the man's face. His beleaguered boss, whose job it was to exemplify the future, had come up against the evil phantoms of workaday reality; he had no choice but to obey the distant commands of the kind of men he saw leading parades in the city streets.

Knollenberg's expression was that of a man starting awake from a dream to find himself surrounded by empty rooms.

'Herr Dudok, I advise you to not to seek Miss Bender's company. She is no longer one of us. A Communist, if you ask me.'

He had not responded. What was there to say? Knollenberg had closed the door behind him, his face white and tense.

In the hours he spent wandering about the factory he had only one thing on his mind. Where was Julia now, and how was he going to shelter her without anybody noticing. What he would do once she was in the flat he did not think about. He suppressed every notion of her physical presence.

'Herr Dudok, the porter has a message for you.'

Knocking on the porter's lodge, he immediately caught sight of a pale-blue envelope lying on the counter. Chr. Dudok, feminine hand. 'To be delivered in person' in the upper left-hand corner.

He read the note as he walked away: 'I can't make eight o'clock, it'll be closer to eleven.' Her message ended with 'Don't worry', in English.

Don't worry. Julia's custom of sprinkling her soft-spoken German with occasional words in English gave their conversations a touch of secrecy and complicity. As it was, though, the phrase only increased his anxiety. But her laconic tone was heartening, as was the fact that she had reached him here, right in the factory. Evidently she had friends she could rely on to deliver messages.

5

It was well past eleven. Chris had been restless all evening. He had tidied his flat: sitting room, kitchen and bedroom were presentable, but no more than that — she was not to think he wanted her to move in. There was no clatter of feet on the pavement outside, no trace of the hectic atmosphere of morning. His window looked onto a street fallen silent. A few lone pedestrians, the occasional car. Most Lübeckers had gone to bed.

It was close to midnight when he saw her feet. He recognized her shoes instantly: low heel, buckle, dark-yellow leather, elegant. He sat motionless in the dark, staring at her legs before his window. He wanted to go out to her, yet hesitated, paralysed by the sight of her feet, of the woman standing there, waiting for him to let her in. He could still back out, pretend he wasn't there, draw up the gangplank, keep quiet. No chance: she was already tapping on his window, two, three sharp taps, brisk, confident of his presence even though the light was not on. A few paces and he was at the front door, the next moment she was inside.

He drew the curtains, switched the light on and took her coat. Julia said nothing, merely looked about her, calmly.

'Sweet of you to wait up for me. It all took a bit longer than I expected. I'm sorry.'

'Where have you been, Julia? Nobody saw you arrive here, did they?'

'No, I made sure of that, you needn't be afraid.'

But he was afraid, afraid for her, afraid of an outside world turning against her, wanting to be rid of her. He looked away when he said that he had made up a bed for her, and that she might be tired and want to sleep.

'Let's talk for a bit, Chris, and a drink would not go amiss, provided you have some whisky, that is.' She was facing the table with the bottle of Jack Daniels, and twisted round to smile at him.

'Where were you off to in such a hurry after the theatre last night? I was going to ask you to join me for a drink, and I called out to you, didn't you hear?'

He had not dared to ask her this when they met earlier in the day, on the café terrace. Her flight through the revolving door of the theatre perturbed him. Julia's pale features lit up by the illuminated sign on the front of the building, the sign with that name — her brother's, as he had since discovered — written in bold capitals. She had paused a moment, looked left and right, then turned to the right, her long coat with the grey fur collar swishing past the tall plate-glass window into the dark.

'I went to see my brother, stayed there all night. They came to arrest him early this morning, but he managed to smuggle me out just in time. I climbed out of a window at the back and dropped into the garden, then over the fence to the neighbours. I know them, they can be trusted. They let me in, so it was quite easy for me to get away.'

'In your fur coat?'

'How did you know I was wearing a fur coat?' She raised her glass to him.

'By noticing someone rushing from the cloakroom ahead of everybody else. Did you really not hear me, or didn't you want to?'

'No, honestly, I didn't hear you, I was in a panic, all I could think of was: I must get hold of Andreas immediately. I was sure they'd come and arrest him, but Andreas wouldn't dream of running away. He said I was exaggerating, that I was being silly and over-protective. He refused to listen. When they came — my God, that was only this morning, it seems an age ago — he said: listen Julia, I'll be fine, just don't try to find me. They were hammering on the door, the bell didn't stop ringing, and then he opened the window at the back and helped me out. He gave me a pat on the neck and whispered 'I love you, my little engineer, off you go now, scram.''

Julia paused, glanced about the room and sat down.

'Nice place. Do you live here alone? Do you have people dropping by, relatives, friends, a girlfriend?'

He shook his head, no, nobody, no landlady, no neighbours, no girlfriend. Thank God for that.

'It's not really safe for you here, though. They're bound to come here sooner or later, and there is no window for you to climb out of. There's just the one door. All they need to do is wait outside, with a police car round the corner.'

On the instant, he regretted his gloom-and-doom scenario. She had been in a panic, she said. Was she in a panic now? Could he be wrong in thinking her cool and collected? No, no girlfriend, thank God. He was reminded of the woman in Holland, hovering in the background these past two years, bent on entrapment. Her fawning and scheming irked him. He felt intimidated, preyed upon by all the attentions and notes she kept sending: a standing invitation to fall in love. Surely she wouldn't take it into her head to pay him an impromptu visit in Lübeck? He discarded the thought as soon as it arose. The Musterbahn was deathly quiet now, no passers-by, no cars, nothing.

'No, Chris, they won't be coming for me just yet. We're not enemies of the state, you know, at least I don't think so. They just don't like actors who direct their own plays. Did you see Andreas staring that Nazi honcho in the face, and then looking right over him into the audience as if he didn't exist? It was fabulous. I was pretty impressed, and so was the man in the front row, so it seems.'

Chris concurred. It had been a crucial moment. The audience in raptures, applause clattering round the auditorium, the lead actor poised all alone on the edge of the stage. His expression was blank, he did not bow, his leap was sudden and impulsive. Andreas Bender seemed to have risen above himself. A giant looming over the lowlife in the front row, about to vent his wrath. Ashen-faced, sweating, cheeks streaked with mascara, shirt open and fluttering, a menacing emissary from an old world that was fast vanishing. The impact of the unspoken curse, Andreas' wordless accusation, his appeal to those who still had a heart. He was up on a soapbox, back on the stage in his parents' sitting room with his sister using two pocket torches as spotlights. He must have felt all the exhilaration and triumph of old, all the rapture and tragedy he knew then. Is it too late? No, ladies and gentlemen, it is not too late. Look at me, here I stand before you, the frightened boy, the lost life, the past imperfect. Get away, be free, ignore this man in black down here before me. The thugs are on the march, do not join them, for pity's sake stop, drop out of the column, run for your life. Andreas Bender, stage director without a script, dazed, worn-out, betrayed. A figure of wax, insubstantial, easily cast aside, no match for the Nazi onslaught. Theatres, stadiums, armies today, and tomorrow the whole world.

'I was afraid they were going to arrest him there and then. I've never seen anything like it, Julia.'

She glanced at him with raised eyebrows, took a sip of her drink, and slowly replaced her glass on the table, each gesture fluent and assured. Chris noted her interrogative look, which showed that she had underestimated how much he was aware of. She had minimized the danger they were in, but it had not escaped him that she and her brother were indeed enemies of the state. Which meant that

56

any friends of theirs would automatically be under suspicion, too, if not under arrest. Offering her a place to stay was risky. Going around with her at all was risky, he perfectly understood that. But he did not care. She was touched by his concern, seemed minded to give him a hug, but she did not.

'Don't look at me like that, Chris. Here, my glass is empty, you might as well pour me another one, while the going's good.'

She did her best to distract him, wishing them to go into the night with some levity. They would have to sleep at some point. Chris felt the moment drawing near; he would not let his thoughts run away with him — he would simply wish her goodnight. He could see Julia making herself small, acting cheerful. In passing she enquired where her bed was, said she would probably be gone by the time he woke up in the morning.

She was a past master at retreat without collateral damage.

Night-time, stillness outside, drowsiness, sleep. Chris pointed her to the alcove behind the kitchen, just big enough to hold a bed. Heard her shift a chair, climb into bed, switch off the light. That she should be right there, in the next room! He did not fall asleep until dawn.

6

Dudok gave a start, did not know where he was for a moment, and began walking. It was not so much walking as shuffling, unaccustomed as he was to the unlit road. He should reach the level crossing at any moment, he reckoned. It was a local line, so he did not expect a train, although one did trundle past when he was within fifty metres of the track. The last train presumably, as it was half past midnight. A few lit compartments, tiny sitting rooms strung together. People gesticulating, a man reading a newspaper, everything pin-sharp against the night. Trains ran slowly on that stretch, and he could not resist counting the carriages as they came past. The modest caravan had a cosy sort of look, inviting even. Except that cosiness had lost all meaning to him.

Dudok plodded on, past the red-and-white checked barrier, across the track. He halted midway to stare after the dwindling rear lights of the train, heard the fading rumble of the carriages going over the sleepers. Years of his life were rolling away, out of sight. How long to reach Lübeck? It was ten hours by rail to

Berlin before the war. Eight hours to Lübeck, he guessed. He had not been back since '38. Not since that desperate night when he went out looking for her, then found her, and lost her again. After which he had fled, his possessions stuffed into a couple of suitcases and a month's rent paid in advance on the off chance that she might have use for his lodgings.

That night, Kristallnacht. The echo of his own name in the first syllable. The remorse had never left him, for allowing himself to be sent home, for not having stayed the course. Those November days of chaos had seen the last glimmers of common decency extinguished. Kristallnacht: it sounded so cheerful, conjuring visions of lavishly decked dinner tables with crystal glasses and burning candles, the epitome of bourgeois *gemütlichkeit*. A misapprehension. There were flames, but not of candles. Dinner tables, chairs, shops, homes, synagogues, Jews. All ready fuel for the con-flagration. The stampede of jackboots in the streets, precisely directed, precisely timed. And the bystanders recoiling into dumb silence, their passiveness never to be redeemed.

Whenever he thought back to that time he remembered himself as a coward. Not that one sole foreigner could have achieved anything. But doing simply nothing, ignoring everything, standing by with hands in pockets and upturned coat collar? He had been out in the streets on the night of November 9th, or rather the early hours of the 10th. Staying indoors had been impossible with the pull of rising tension outside, the running and chasing past his basement window, the shouting, the banging against his wall. It was two in the morning, pitch dark and very cold. He had shut the door behind him and headed off, though not in the same direction as the gangs of overexcited stormtroopers and S.S. youths, chanting menacingly *en route* to some festival of hatred and revenge. The skyline glowed with distant burning, looking over his shoulder he saw yet more fires. He sped to the house Julia had told him about, next to where her brother Andreas lived. He dared to ring the bell, the whole neighbourhood was awake, no-one slept. Julia was not there; she had left the previous day without saying where to. No wonder: she was on the run, did not make appointments, covered her tracks. Chris had managed to keep in touch after a fashion, because she needed him. And loved him? Sometimes he thought she did, sometimes he was sure, sometimes he had no idea.

The brown battalions, Horst Wessel everywhere, all along the streets, into the synagogues. What a blaze! Never were their flags raised higher, never their steps calmer. Well, not so calm maybe. Chris pushed through the people on the pavement, back to his rooms. Without Julia, without hope.

Now he had seen and heard the fury for himself. Pyromaniacs and gunmen in chorus, singing of the day of bread and freedom that was dawning. They sang as they left the scenes of devastation and plunder; they chanted and yelled and roared as they closed their ranks in tight formation.

He had gone past every place they had ever been together. He had banged on the door of Grand-Café Elzas, peered through the window at their table. She was not there.

The last metres to his front door, five a.m., staggering with exhaustion. Then he saw her, leaning against his doorpost, barely recognizable in her long dark overcoat, a woollen hat pulled over her ears. Just standing there, saying nothing, looking at him. He wanted to yell at her, he wanted to shout that he had been looking for her everywhere and where the hell had she been.

'Oh, there you are,' was all he said.

He drew her into the flat, helped her out of her coat, took her hat. In the dark, with muffled sounds from outside, furniture stolidly in position, their world narrowed into their embrace. Her hand on the back of his

61

head, her cheek cupped in his hand, throbbing stillness, spreading warmth. A night like no other, a daybreak like no other. Arson and murder had been cried and perpetrated without resistance. Arson and murder were the watchwords, the code. Love had been driven underground, into warrens, alcoves and unlit rented rooms.

Chris and Julia lay in each other's arms, silent and mindless. They watched as the light of day crept up on them, reaching their faces. Sleep was for the unthinking, for those who had jobs to go to, for Knollenberg and his engineers, for the storm-troopers and their campaign of destruction. They did not speak, for they had no words. Only when she made to leave, only then had she spoken. Her sentence could not have been harsher.

'Get away, Chris, you must get away as soon as you can. Go back home. I'll manage, I can't leave now, and besides, I don't want to.'

'Come with me to Holland, Julia. You should come with me.'

'One day perhaps, but not just yet. Promise me you'll catch the first train to Holland, do it today. I mean it. Don't try to get in touch with me. You must go at once, Chris, or you'll be putting me at risk.'

The tremor of an axe on a chopping block.

He made no attempt to oppose her, only held her close, stroked her hair, her eyebrows. She laid her finger on his lips.

Then she walked away, glancing back over her shoulder. And he said, 'I love you, my little engineer.'

Her saddest smile was the response.

7

The return by train. There was no return. There was only flight, defeat, horror, animal longing. He did not even have a photograph of her; he would have to make do with the memory of her hands, her dark eyebrows, how he traced them with his fingertips, her hand stroking his shoulder, her breath on his neck. A magic box full of gestures to take on his journey homeward. There would be no arrival for him, ever again.

By the time the train departed the following morning, promptly at seven, he was dead tired. He had left his basement with hurried, quiet steps, having made the arrangements with his boss in the hours after Julia had left him, not by cycling over to Lubecawerke but by telephone. He had asked to be remembered to his colleagues at the office. Knollenberg had not even seemed surprised, on the contrary, he sounded curiously sympathetic, even a touch concerned. Would he please convey his regards to Herr Dudok senior? He hoped to see Chris again soon, in good health, and wished him all the best for the future.

He had caught the first available train to Holland. Lübeck station was a miniature palace in brick, with green turrets and an undulating roof projecting from the wall above tall, arched windows. There was no sign of recent turmoil, not the slightest indication of catastrophe, nothing recalling orchestrated plunder. In the gathering light he saw a bluish haze over the Old Town, with the steeples of the Marienkirche rising high above the houses.

He had ached all over during the short walk from the Musterbahn to the station. Down the Mühlen Strasse, already bustling at this hour, past the crossroads at the Kohlmarkt, where he and Julia had sat and talked on a café terrace — but he refused to look. Past Grand-Café Elzas — he looked away. Past the accursed Holstentor, where the brownshirts mustered for their parades. Struggling with his luggage, having to stop frequently to draw breath, keeping his eyes on the ground. He had wished to look and see as little as possible.

'Get away as soon as you can, Chris, or you'll be putting me at risk.'

So where was the risk? Where? Trains were running to schedule, paperboys plied their trade, shops were opening for business. A well-oiled machine in perfect order, no hitches, no delays, nobody stopping him. A respectable-looking foreigner returning home. A time bomb. Four years later the Old Town would be gone, pulverized, laid waste, the Grand-Café razed to the ground.

The steeples above the Old Town would have been visible from the train for some time, had he wished to see them. But he averted his face from the window: the view was more than he could bear. At the approach of each station he resolved to get off, turn back, make a stand. But he did nothing, and the hours ground onward. For as long as he was on German soil he jumped each time the door of his compartment slid open.

'You'll be putting me at risk, Chris,' an endless refrain to the rhythmic throb of carriage wheels. The nearer he drew to Holland the more he wondered whether he had heard her correctly. Had she really said that, or was it his imagination? Or had she sent him away because she doubted him? Not his love so much, but perhaps she found him weak, lacking in drive and confidence. He was a bind to her, asked too many questions, made too many demands. He had got it all wrong: she must have meant that he would be putting her at risk because he slowed her down, impaired her freedom. She was not after anything permanent. She wanted to protect herself; all the attention he lavished on her, his love for her, only drove her into a corner. Her Germany had no place for him, couldn't he see that? Go away, Chris, forget all this.

But what about her hands, then, and her eyes, and the timeless moment of their embrace? His uncertainty ended there, the early morning after the flames, with Julia's wordless answer.

He still felt exhausted when the train drew into the town where his parents lived, where the factory was. The wind ruffled his hair as he stepped down to the platform, unnoticed by anyone but a station porter eager for custom. It was three o'clock on 11 November, 1938. He felt stiff from the long train journey, and was hard put to keep up with the porter pushing the handcart with his luggage. In single file, as if he were being taken into custody along with his personal effects. That was what it felt like: being taken into custody. And what it became was solitary confinement.

Where were they now, those philosophers of his? Where were the heroes of the *Verneinung*, the champions of denial and negation? Pillars of support for a sorry, estranged lad shambling through the wings of history, looking about in despair for a lost love. Julia was tougher than all those system builders and wordsmiths put together. Again he was overcome by the old, baffling sense of emptiness, a waif in a lost land. He was barely able to put the feeling into words, it defied description: he was there and he was not.

Chris shuddered at his thoughts as he approached the exit. If only he were a station porter, if only he were the train driver returning to Lübeck, if only he were with Julia. He went through the park opposite the station, to his parents' house, to the questions in their eyes. There would be no answers. That he had fled, was nobody else's business.

8

Dudok stood at the level-crossing, unnoticed by the passengers heading off into the night. His last night.

The train passed from view; he caught the faint jingle of the warning bell in the far distance. Trundling onwards, all those people with a goal in life.

He gathered himself to walk on. It was hardly walking, more a matter of limbs in mechanical motion. The path led to his house, he could not miss it. Van Dijk would likely as not be at home with his wife by now. His much-prized Wolseley under lock and key. The diary lying in the back — no harm in that, surely? He tried to think whether there was anything in it that might give people ideas later on. He thought not. He never mentioned Julia, not even in his most private jottings.

She would vanish along with him. Never had she been closer to him than in these last weeks. There had been years in which he had managed to keep her at bay by consigning her to the recesses of his memory, but always for a time, never for long. She kept resurfacing, bringing everything to a standstill, making the most ordinary of actions extraordinary and unfeasible. Such as walking, walking in an unlit landscape as he was doing now. Lurching, more like. He stopped again, needed to get his breath back, find his bearings. He peered in the direction he imagined his house to be.

Whoever was has no house now, will never build one . . .

A church bell struck one. The first hour of this Sunday was over. It was all set, today was the day. He had put it off once before; he would not let that happen again. It was not worth it. He could not go on like this, there was to be no more stumbling about, no more mindless muttering, no more empty skies.

'Hello, Meneer Dudok!' The girl on the bicycle appeared out of nowhere: Lottie, the neighbours' daughter, a mere seventeen, on her way home to bed. 'You're out late.'

'It is the heat. I felt like taking a stroll, but it is pitch dark out here. Could you shine your bike lamp on my path a little way, or I shall never get back.'

'Are you sure you're alright, Meneer Dudok?'

'I'm quite alright, my dear, just fine.' Such a sweet girl. He wished all the best for her, and felt an urgent desire to include her in his

70

will. Well, he could always put something down on paper later on, some sort of bequest. Was that feasible? No, it would have to be done via the notary, of course, so it was too late for that now. The girl would be mystified; besides, her parents would find it suspicious. How were they to know how gratifying it was on a night like this to have one's path lit up by a sweet-natured, soft-spoken young girl.

He held one end of the handlebar, she the other, with the bicycle between them, the lamp glowing like the tip of a cigarette, the dynamo slurring against the tyre. She steered him effortlessly to De Venhorst. They turned into the drive, where the gravel crunched under the wheels.

'Are you often out this late?'

'Late? This is early for me, Meneer Dudok. It's just because I have to be up again at six, as we're going on holiday.'

It was good to hear that his neighbours would be away, very good. It would be a couple of weeks before they heard; all done and dusted by then, everything back to normal.

'Where do you go when you go out?'

'Over to the Helios, mostly. It's a nice place, and there's dancing until three in the morning.'

'Do you dance with all the boys, or with a

few, or just with one maybe?'

'Just one, Meneer Dudok. It's been a few months now, which is not like me at all, but he's great fun.'

Dudok made no comment. He lowered himself onto a wicker chair near the fen, then asked if she would mind keeping him company for a bit, 'seeing as it's not that late'. The house was deathly quiet, the night was warm, he had no wish to go indoors just yet. The neighbours' daughter eyed him with curiosity. He was able to see that thanks to the light over the front door. Van Dijk had switched it on earlier. The lights were on upstairs, too. The curtains were open, but the locked house looking singularly uninviting to him, repellent even.

'Tell me what it's like at that Helios club of yours. So there's dancing, but what else do you do?'

'We drink wine, we smoke, we chat, and then there's the music. Nothing special. It's always jam-packed, you can hardly hear what anyone's saying, so I wouldn't go there if I were you.'

He smiled; the notion was comical. Lottie thought so too, because she laughed out loud. Midges hovered in little clusters above the water.

'A bit like that, Meneer Dudok, like those

midges over there, dancing and bunching together. Look, that's me, dancing with Mark.' She pointed into the dark.

Dudok looked. He saw her painted fingernails, the plain gold bangle on her wrist.

'Is that his name then — Mark?' He wanted to keep the conversation going, fill the hours.

'Mark Blinkert, he's a drama student, but he's already been in a couple of television series. Do you watch television at all, have you ever seen him?'

He shook his head.

'He had a small part in a war film recently. A Dutch fighter pilot *en route* to Germany — did you know they bombed whole cities to smithereens during the night?'

He was aware of that. Very aware. Lübeck. It was always the same, just as he thought everything was safely buried under an unmoveable slab of Dutch reinforced concrete, Lübeck came rushing to mind. Always in troubled times, as when his wife was ill and then died. And always their Kristallnacht, their shattered fate.

His wife lay dying, but he had been unable to focus his attention, however hard he tried. During his sickroom vigils beside her shrivelled body, Julia had shamelessly loomed over him.

Some days after the cremation Van Dijk drove him to Ellecom, the urn beside him on the back seat, the engine purring discreetly. It was November, chill weather, fallen leaves as far as the eye could see. Van Dijk drove at a snail's pace, in fourth gear, as though in imitation of a funeral cortège. Which of course it was.

The Ellecom graveyard, what could be finer than that? Dudok was fond of it; his father and mother were buried there, and he had long since reserved a plot for himself and his wife. He had not reckoned with her predeceasing him, let alone with her wish to be cremated. So that left rather a lot of space for him. Well then, he would share it with the urn.

From afar they spotted a workman among the tombstones. No doubt the person responsible for preparing the burial. Van Dijk parked the car just off the main road. They had to go up a sloping footpath, across the railway track, and there, on the other side, lay the small cemetery. Two weeping beeches, a few lanes with graves on either side, a hedge, a boundary wall with a gate.

Anyone setting foot in that place became instantly reconciled with death. There was something positively appealing about it, with the wooded area beyond, the trains passing by, and the scent of nature all around.

Dudok and Van Dijk. Van Dijk carrying the urn. Up the slope in silence, through the gate in silence, side by side towards the open grave.

'Go on then, Van Dijk.'

Just then a train rattled past, and Van Dijk gestured that he had not heard. Nor did he make to climb down into the hole, which was remarkably deep. Dudok held on to his hat, the wind gusted over the graves. When the train had gone Van Dijk threw him a questioning look. Dudok stared ahead.

'Would you prefer to place it there yourself, sir?'

He did not answer.

The way she had stood leaning against the door in the near-light of five in the morning. Her expression quizzical and dark at the same time. The inexorable moment of preparing for their embrace, there on the doorstep of his Lübeck home. The basement flat empty, waiting for them to come down and find love. Love until sunrise.

'No, I would rather you did it, Van Dijk — my hip.'

'Been wrestling with angels, I shouldn't wonder,' muttered Van Dijk, with unwitting aptness, for all that Dudok's angel was of different provenance.

Julia floated in and out of his consciousness, then and so many times thereafter, there
was no escape. All those months of living
towards that moment, going round in circles,
longing, hoping, banishing the thought and
going after it again. In her arms at last, her
hand round his hip at last. Six o'clock, seven,
eight, first light, and slowly they disentangled
themselves. Clothes, where were their clothes,
what was the time, was that someone at the
door, no, not yet.

The Musterbahn began to hum, later than
usual it seemed, whereas it was Thursday, a
normal weekday. Mass tiredness? Jews rounded
up? Shops wrecked? Synagogues pillaged, by
any chance? And who had overslept, who had
stayed up until the early hours, who had thought
of the Rubicon being crossed, the die cast, the
genie let out of the bottle? Julia and Chris,
they had thought of those things. They were a
perfect fit, seamless, as light as a feather, the
world in ruination all around them.

Van Dijk, the urn clamped under his arm,
flexed his knees and awkwardly slithered down
into the grave, a large concrete box with enough
room for two coffins. Too much room. He
looked up uncertainly. Stifling a smile, Dudok
clasped his thigh.

'A little more to the left, Van Dijk, you want
to leave some space for me, remember.'

Jovial, in his way. As Van Dijk climbed back out of the concrete box, Dudok asked him to wait a while, as he wished to walk a little. To walk Julia away, get rid of the bad taste of thinking of her now, in this place.

Dudok strolled along the graves, his parents resting beneath their slate-grey slab, a grave like his own. The place was well maintained — who by, he wondered. He went up some steps to a wide circle of gravel with a weeping beech in the centre. He read the inscription on a cross of white marble: 'We are in favour with our Lord.' What was that supposed to mean? Jumping the queue no doubt. He found it distasteful. The long lane of gravel bisecting the cemetery branched out into several paths winding among the oldest tombs. 'Blessed be the child whose destiny brings it sooner to God.' Epitaph of a twelve-year-old girl, how wonderfully crude. He felt chilly; dusk was beginning to fall. Time to head back.

The neighbours' daughter looked at her watch.

'I promised my parents I'd be back on time, and I'm already later than I said I'd be. I really ought to go now, Meneer Dudok.'

'I quite understand, my dear. You have been very kind. Please give my regards to your parents. When will you be back, Lottie?'

77

'In a fortnight. I'll drop by and tell you all about it.'

'And have fun with Mark.'

She laughed and took up her bike. He saw her give a little wave before being engulfed by the dark.

9

The *Heyligenstaedt* — she's been found! towed all the way to the Baltic, apparently, and put ashore at the harbour of Travemünde.

September 1945, and Chris Dudok was the owner of a factory stripped and laid waste. The *Heyligenstaedt* was their most beloved machine, a huge turning lathe, the mainstay of production. Seized by the Jerries in '44, along with everything else they fancied. Losing the lathe had been calamitous. They were decapitated, trade was wiped out. What little they had left was worthless.

The months following the liberation were far from easy. Naturally, they had celebrated during those first weeks of warm weather in May and June: they were excited and relieved. And poor. Chris ferried himself across the canal to the factory each day to see who had returned from the war.

The majority of his workforce had been rounded up and deported to Germany. More men turned up each day, swelling the ranks of those hoping for work that was not on offer. There were no machines, there was no money and there were no orders. When would he have to close down?

He began to dread going across. The old self-service ferry was moored close by, diagonally opposite the factory. A machine factory no more. Empty warehouses, desolate halls, dilapidated staffrooms; his heart sank each time he entered his office. His desk was bare. To be sure, they were free, the occupier gone, the hated Germans sent packing. Now for the recovery of their possessions.

Then came the news — *Heyligenstaedt found!* — a telegram from one of his father's contacts in Germany. He wanted to clap someone on the shoulder, saw no-one, ran outside, wanted to raise the flag. He ferried himself back to the other side and a moment later flung his arms about his wife.

'This will be a new beginning! We can get cracking at last, show them what we're made of!' It was a rare outburst of joy, his first hope in years. And all because of a machine, a dumb clump of iron. He knew they would win through now, getting that clump of iron back was merely their first victory.

His wife hugged him again and again: 'It'll be like the old days, Dude. And maybe, maybe we could start . . . ' she paused a moment before deftly completing her sentence: 'getting some orders in.' They were childless, and would remain so.

Exactly one year after his return from Lübeck they were married. On his harsh terms: there were to be no children. He would never inflict this world on another human being. Never.

She had given him her promise, thinking she would find some way of changing his mind. 'Never' sounded so final. She would take him by the hand and lead him, seduce him, mislead him if necessary. A child would arrive in due course. But it was all taking too long, the war had only hardened his conviction that he was right, and she could feel her hopes of motherhood slowly but surely being stifled to extinction. By the years of proximity to him, by his ineptitude, by his taciturn ways.

There was a degree of reticence about everything he said and did. She could not understand where it came from, and sometimes thought he was hiding something from her, something to do with that year he spent in Lübeck, probably. He had already shown a streak of sarcasm before he left, as well as a fondness for gloomy writers, but he had also been more cheerful and outgoing. It was that dark side of his lit up by his vulnerable charm that she had found compelling. She could not make him out, which only fired her interest.

They had been to Budapest and Paris, they had gone sailing, they had driven to parties in an open convertible, they had danced. But he had always kept her at a polite remove; no question of an easy conquest. It had been a long year of sidling up to him. And then he had slunk away to Lübeck, Germany. Without much explanation, without much emotion, and without her.

'Our lathe is over in Travemünde, so it will be a while before we get her back,' he said, tempering his own enthusiasm. How had that thing landed there, of all places?

Travemünde, summer of '38. Sundays at the beach, chair firmly planted in the sand, books to read, boys selling tea and beer. Julia had gone away that summer, he did not know where. He had spent one single day with her, when they met at the seaside in late August. She had left a note for him with the porter at Lubecawerke: 'Sunday, eleven a.m., Travemünde, Café Seetempel.'

He had arrived there at ten, hoping she might be early. Twelve o'clock, one, it was not until half past one that she appeared. He saw her coming across the long stretch of grass, dressed for summer and wearing a sun hat, a pale pink scarf around her bare shoulders, and her favourite yellow shoes with the buckles. He raised his hand to beckon her, but she had already spotted him. Overcome with joy, he asked no questions, gave no indication of his anxiety.

'Hello, Chris, enjoying the health resort are you?'

'Not enough pretty nurses around, and too much waiting.'

She gave a mock salute. 'Message received and understood, Cap'n. It won't happen again.'

And it did not happen again.

There was indeed something of the spa about the place, with the cream of Lübeck society gathering around the open-air dance floors, orchestras vying for attention, saloon cars delivering lavishly dressed ladies and gentlemen in black ties, yachts at anchor offshore, the occasional seaplane landing on the waves. Barely a uniform to be seen, as though the coast had been magically exempted from the iron discipline pervading the country. The regime of the sun, tomorrow did not exist, strike up the violins. Out here on the Baltic shore you would have thought the very notion of war had been banned.

Café-Restaurant Seetempel, flag flying, stood on a promontory of rock overlooking the sea. Germany's furthermost point, two more steps and they would drop off the continent, free of the insanity encroaching on all sides. The radio man was a disaster, worse than Chris had initially believed. As for the never-ending palavers in Holland, the stultifying compromises, the wavering, all that was better than falling for the great lie of the national soul, the fixation on a mythical perception of blood and soil, the idiocy of one group being held superior to another. It was nauseating, loathsome, and also frightening.

He stood up, unsure whether he might kiss her, took her hand and raised it to his lips. She looked down on his bowed head, the dark hair smoothed back. The next moment they were sharing a table on a crowded terrace with waiters silently passing by. She had brought a book, which she laid on the chair beside her. Shiny cover, Rilke, *Das Buch der Bilder*. They said little, drank their glasses of fruit juice. He ordered white wine, suggested a bite to eat. The tablecloth billowed in the breeze, gulls sailed lazily overhead, all seemed right with the world.

That afternoon became lodged in his memory as the gentlest, most luminous he had ever known.

'Where have you been these past weeks, Julia?' He tried to put the question as casually as possible.

'With some friends of my brother's in the

84

Black Forest. I thought it would be good to lie low for a bit, and you can do that there. I had no idea there were still such remote villages in Germany, people just carrying on with their lives and not being at all impressed by what's happening in Berlin.'

She had gone hoping to find out more about her brother's fate, hoping for clues by way of his friends. Buchenwald, the name had a romantic sound. It was not far from Weimar, once the town of Goethe and Schiller, but since fallen under the tyranny of the lash. There were strange goings-on there, dark rumours, but that was all she had gleaned from her expedition.

Brother and sister, forcibly parted yet close in spirit, Andreas imprisoned and Julia leading a roaming existence.

She had also been to Weimar. No news there either, unsurprisingly. She had wandered about a bit, and had seen the camp from far off. Innocent-looking barracks, sunshine, nothing special. So that was presumably where Andreas was being held, although she found it impossible to grasp. How could he be so near and yet so utterly out of reach?

'That last conversation we had, Andreas and I, that night after the performance — it hasn't stopped, you know, I just keep on talking to him. Which is very pleasant, really. Our whole childhood comes alive, our shamelessly happy childhood. At any rate until our parents died, because after that things were different. But the foundation of happiness is as firm as ever, thanks to the constant patter of our young feet, I suppose.'

Her story came out in fits and starts, nuggets that Chris would treasure.

That early morning in Lübeck, at Andreas' lodgings in the middle of the Dom quarter, she had heard the boots from afar. The acoustics in the narrow streets, while not conducive to sleep, were providential to anyone on the alert.

'Did I tell you how extraordinarily efficient Andreas was? He grabbed my coat, hid my glass and the ashtray in the cupboard and slid me right out of the window, all in one swoop. Curtains, quicker than scat. The perfect stagehand. I miss him. I miss his voice, and his fierce eyes.'

'They're bound to let him go, Julia. They haven't even trumped up charges against him.'

'They don't need to, Chris. Bringing charges is old-fashioned. People are being shunted off to camps all the time, but until now nobody seems to be getting out. I'm just trying to keep up my spirits. I've written to him a few times, but I doubt he's receiving my letters. Friends of mine in Weimar have promised to let me know as soon as they hear anything.'

They sauntered back to Travemünde along the seafront. The beach down below was dotted with seemingly happy families. The end of the holiday season, August wearing thin. Chris kept looking at her from the corner of his eyes, fighting the urge to take her hand. She seemed not to notice. She talked, fell silent, talked some more, asked him how his summer had been. Now and then her arm brushed against his, she stopped a few times to tap him on the shoulder and point something out. It was late afternoon when they reached the harbour, which was bustling with animation, strains of music drifting towards them from different directions. Singular hours, without perspective, without end. A sense of total safety possessed him, bewildering though it was.

He would not give her the opportunity to make a dash for the train. He had seen a café near the station, and before she could say anything he drew her inside. It was not busy. Most people were still sitting on the beach or strolling ostentatiously along the shoreline. Wicker chairs and tables interspersed with potted palms, a little orchestra playing, the usual Sunday afternoon ambience, no sign of any trouble. *Was* there any trouble? How could there be? Bright sunshine, calm sea, gentle breeze, strolling men and women sporting healthy tans. Sunday respite from the weekday calls for action. Peace reigning supreme by the sea, a place where children paddled canoes, where boys went sailing and girls huddled together to gossip. Sheer normality, utter contentment.

Straw hat, straw fire, last straw, charade. Andreas would have played it to the hilt, better than anyone there, he would have been the perfect gentleman on a Sunday outing, the self-assured man in the summer jacket and yellow waistcoat consulting his fob watch with the train schedule at the back of his mind, his arm circling his wife's waist, genial, effusive, bolder and freer than normal. Andreas would have impersonated the entire family, husband, wife, sons and daughters and in-laws. Hopping, whistling, swaggering, singing, clapping, falling, forgetting himself.

Andreas. He was sitting there with them.

Julia kept steering the conversation to him. Chris could hear the undertow of anxiety in her ironic stance.

'My God, Chris, to think how he loathed tidying up, shining shoes, making beds, things like that. Apparently you can get a fortnight's aggravated arrest for a button missing on your coat, they put you on bread and water for the slightest thing. Poor Andreas, he must miss me terribly. I used to do a lot of that stuff for him.'

Aggravated arrest, bread and water, notions and terms from another world, like the rumble of thunder far away in the dark domain of hearsay. Not wanting their day to end in gloomy conjecture, Chris tried to divert her attention to stories of her childhood. But she was losing heart. She kept breaking off, grew restless, her eyes shifting nervously. Chris could feel that it was time for her to go.

'We can't travel back together, Chris. You'd better wait here for an hour or so, then I can get a head start. I'll be in touch. How is Knollenberg, by the way?'

'Retreated into his shell, ever since the day he sacked you. Grumpier than before, but, oddly enough, friendlier towards me.'

'You'll give him my regards, won't you?' She smiled, looked at him, her face flushed with a touch of sunburn. It was getting late, the heat was abating, the sun stood low in the sky. He could no longer think of anything to prevent her from leaving.

He would stay behind, on his own, yes, she had made herself quite clear. Whatever you say, Julia, I'll wait here another hour, don't you fret. A whole witless, feeble, cowardly hour of being deprived of your company. Go on, then, take your gloves and your shawl, but leave your handbag I beseech you, so you'll have to come back for it.

'Take care, Julia,' he said, with more emphasis than he intended. She was not to notice how scared he was. 'When do you think we can go for another walk?'

'I'd like to say every Sunday, but I can't, unfortunately. I'm leaving for Weimar tomorrow, can't say exactly when I'll be back. But I'll let you know as soon as possible.'

She brushed her cheek against his, clasped his hand and quickly let go. Striding past the window, her shawl fluttering behind her, she threw him a glance. He nodded, so did she. Then she was gone.

10

Chris had crossed over to the factory earlier than usual, accompanied by his wife. All the workers were there, most accompanied by their wives, some with their children as well. The *Heyligenstaedt* was to arrive that morning, after days of arduous transport. Overland across the bombed-out wasteland of northern Germany, then by barge along the waterways of Holland. *Heyligenstaedt:* what a name for an inanimate object made of nuts and bolts. But rarely had a machine been given a grander welcome. The 'state of holiness' implied by the name inspired all alike, as though it had been invented for this very day.

Change was upon them, the first hurdle had been cleared. The big entrance doors stood wide open, the walls were decked with bunting and the flag was flying, even though that was not officially permitted.

'Meneer Chris! She's on her way!' shouted one of the lathe operators — she was *their* machine, their very own turning lathe, worked by them for so many years. Cutting, de-burring, polishing — without the lathe the factory was nothing. The *Heyligenstaedt* was the jewel in the crown, the nerve at the centre.

'Meneer Chris.' The term of address jarred with him; he could never get used to it. Who on earth had come up with it? His father had been Meneer Dudok, he had simply been Chris initially, but at sixteen he had become Meneer Chris. Doomed to succeed his father. He had gone to university to get away from the whole idea for a spell. No more than a detour, an interlude, a postponement.

His year in Germany had been the only year that really counted, his baptism of fire, his near-successful escape. Followed by a shamefaced return. Back in the bosom of the family, he had been at the mercy of the eager girlfriend. She was impossible to avoid, and after a time her unflagging energy and cheerful disposition began to take effect.

A greater contrast with Julia did not exist. It was not until much later that he realized how rigorously he had tried to erase every reminder of her. He had to create a life for himself in which she did not figure. The most tenuous of associations, the remotest resemblance in voice, tone, glance, facial expression, would be intolerable. His wife would have to be her diametric opposite. He had to barricade his past. Not that it would take any notice.

The men in the factory began to cheer; they poured outside to welcome the barge bringing their repossessed machine. As when the Canadian troops came to liberate them, such was the clamour and jubilation. A foreman stood on deck waving a flag, the barge horn sounded unremittingly, mounted police held the traffic at bay. All those months of dreaming and speculating, and now the big day had finally arrived. A crane hoisted the lathe off the barge and set it down in its rightful place at the centre of the hall: the spider restored to her web, sprung for action. And action there would be — Meneer Chris had told them so.

'A speech, Meneer Chris! Speech, speech!'

It was inescapable. He would speak. There was a hush of suspense in the crowded hall. He had nothing prepared, and stood before them with an almost helpless air, as though his words were coming from elsewhere. He spoke of the war, of the long years of persecution and extortion, of the joy of liberation and the return of so many from Germany. The factory would be resurrected, with so much of Europe in ruins their machines would be indispensable for the reconstruction of industry.

'My friends, I have the profoundest admiration for your loyalty and resilience.

Only four months ago this hall was a wasteland. Storerooms bare, offices empty. But our turning lathe is back where she belongs, the first orders are lying on my desk, we are all set to go, and we shall never stop. I thank every one of you from the bottom of my heart. Thank you.'

Applause ensued, three hurrahs, more speeches, then drinks of *genever* and savouries all round, children playing hide-and-seek, women lapsing into relieved chatter.

That night Chris woke several times feeling breathless and hot, as though lying in the sun on a beach. In his half-sleep he relived the day's festivities, vague unfinished conversations, things he had wanted to say and only occurred to him now. His wife lay at arm's length beside him. At five o'clock he got up, dressed, and left the house. It was no longer dark, but the sun had not yet risen. Without premeditation, he made for the old ferry and pulled himself along the steel cable to the other side. He was his own ferryman. He saw no-one, only the calm ripples in his wake. Peaceful water, kindly, obliging water.

He unlocked the factory door, stepped inside, took a chair and placed it beside the *Heyligenstaedt*.

Ten past five. He raised his hand to his neck, noticed that he was sweating. Not from exertion, he thought, rather from the strain of suppressing his fear.

He had fallen again during the night, an endless drop into nothing and nowhere. His fall was ineluctable; it was a recurring dream, and had been since childhood. The sensation was not disagreeable, even the desolation that went with it possessed a certain sweetness.

The quiet in the hall resembled that of an old church. Every sound was sucked up into the elevation. Two cranes loomed overhead, their long chains reaching to the ground. The great lathe at his side was an apparatus whose workings he understood in theory but not in practice. There was not a single machine he knew how to operate, he did not have the right kind of hands. His clothes were wrong, too. He would have been alright milking cows, at a pinch. Haymaking, harrowing the fields, hitching horses — no problem. Each time he returned home to the city his grandfather had shaken his head: 'Poor lad, nothing doing there.'

Among his books he had forgotten his hands, but among his machines he lost all sense of life. Metallic world, the sound of hammers and welding machines, the scream of the circular saws and the drills, the unrelenting crash of steel on steel.

He leaned back against the lathe and

looked about him. The stillness was oppressive. The whole factory seemed to be keeping a deliberate silence, the hush expectant to a degree he had never experienced before. There stood the first of their drum dryers, ready for finishing on the lathe, the silvery hood gleaming in the receding dusk. Looking up he saw two pigeons roosting side by side on a crossbeam. Someone had obviously left a window open.

The euphoria of the previous day was over. His words in celebration of their precious machine sounded hollow to him now. But the rousing cheers in response had lifted him up momentarily, emboldening him to an unprecedented degree. He had actually fired up his men, in a way: he had raised his voice, foretold the future, declared that their factory would flourish and that the desert would bloom like a rose. Throwing his inborn caution to the winds, acting the bringer of good fortune — what had come over him?

The let-down had not been long in coming: it had assailed him that same night.

He became aware of the chill in the factory hall. He shivered, but not from the cold, because his shirt was clammy against the back of his chair. He wondered if he was ill.

He was worn out, thirty-seven, with the future turning the screws on his throat.

Liberation by all means, new perspectives, new orders, Europe today and tomorrow the whole world. He was as much at a loss in his own home as in his executive office among wage records and contract briefs. Prosperity would return sooner or later, there was no doubt about that — the pre-war lifestyle would be restored. Motoring trips, the Flanders coast, Capri, his wife's wishes would be fulfilled. All but one.

His father had died during the war. Hardly the death of a hero: fallen off his bicycle during a trip to the countryside in search of food. Heart failure. Perhaps heroic after all. Found by a farmer he knew from the old days, lying in the yard, his spectacles still on his nose, the lenses broken. Butter and ham and potatoes in a sack by his side. In his letters to Lübeck his father had already warned that he would not last much longer. That first letter telling him that he, Chris, would have to take over at the factory — it had knocked the breath out of him. He had left his basement to go and sit by the water-side round the corner from the Musterbahn.

The letter had reached him on a Saturday afternoon, soon after his return from the office. It was the dead of winter, early January, the river was frozen, with ducks jostling in the remaining open water, with yesterday's snow on the ground and a leaden sky. The perfect décor for bad tidings, as far as he was concerned. Dark red-brick cathedral at his back, leafless trees and bushes on either side. He felt numb. He could not believe his father was ill, there had never been anything wrong with him. A quiet man, seldom angry, seldom tiresome, forever at his factory. But also a man with clear-cut views of his son's career, adamant that Chris should succeed him — he was made of the right stuff, and besides his younger brother was far too young. The cathedral bells began to peal, guard dogs of an invisible master. The volume of sound was startling. Twisting round, he saw a wedding party emerging from the cathedral, the groom in uniform with a swastika armband, the bride in white. A sorry sight on a soulless Saturday afternoon, at an hour when people had no business getting married, not here, not in this day and age. For a moment he was distracted from the news that would haunt him for months to come. The marriage bond, personified on those cathedral steps, cast him into a deep gloom.

The ducks in the open water in front of him grew restive in the persistent clanging of bells, then took off in swift succession. The newly wed couple proceeded past. Gross-looking bride and groom, gross-looking kinsfolk in their wake. He felt uneasy observing them, there was a certain hostility about their little parade.

Parades were never a good sign: there was always the intimation of an onward march towards iniquity, deliberate, eager, warlike. He had seen and heard more than enough parades since his arrival. Germany sang, so woe betide. Even a wedding cortège of forty could spell trouble; more often than not it would harbour several uniforms.

His father's letter had been the watershed. Until then he had persuaded himself that his future still lay open. Lübeck had been nothing but a stay of execution, he now realized. He had asked his father to mediate for him: his wish to go abroad, get some experience, take a side road from the straight and narrow of the family firm, a break from the girl trailing her bait of subtle niceties. Ah, a year in Lübeck! He had pulled it off, new freedom, new horizons. Until the postman delivered the letter. The din in the bell towers ebbed away. The small square was deserted once more; the brick walls of the museum adjoining the church loomed forbiddingly. Chris longed to fling the letter into the open water and run away, take the train home and tell his father to find somebody else to run the company. Not him, not just yet, he needed to travel first, wake up in other countries, read, and think. He was not ready to go home, to get married and settle down, to give congratulatory speeches to people for a lifetime of work. Father, please get better, there can't be anything wrong with you, you were never ill, only a bit quiet these last years. Who said your health is failing, which doctor examined you, how can they tell anyway?

But he remained where he was, sitting motionless with the letter in his hand. The ducks alighted again, back on their home ground. A light snow began to fall.

The Musterbahn dissolved, the winter evaporated, it was late August, the early hour was chill and bleak, the factory hall depopulated. Chris sat very still, afraid to rouse the pigeons, or himself maybe. The emptiness all around was curiously soothing to him. He knew perfectly well what his wife was about to say when he told her about the *Heyligenstaedt* being found.

'We might start . . . '

Her hesitation had been too obvious, she had changed the subject a fraction too late, she had come within one word of expressing her wish. Infected by his enthusiasm, she had promptly envisaged giving birth. But he was never unprepared, he never engaged with her on the spur of the moment, he knew her

100

monthly cycle, he was the infallible calculator of her fertility. They were both on the wrong side of thirty. It would not happen, for all that she hoped against hope.

Chris knew he had made the right decision. The dereliction, the betrayal, the massacres, who would wish to grow up with such a past looming over you? That was not how he put it to his wife, though. He was less blunt. But the sentiment leaked into his every thought, his every word: endless variations of the same extenuated fear and apprehension. He imagined the peaceful water of the canal. Why shouldn't he do as so many others had done before him? What luxury to wash his hands of it all. His brother was making excellent progress, his sister needed no help from him, there was only his wife. She was the obstacle.

His mind drifted on. The cold crept up on him, and he thought of the strong, steel cable along which the ferry was propelled, then of the chain hanging down from the crane, within easy reach, surely there was some way . . .

The main door of the hall burst open, startling the pigeons. Two lathe operators strode towards their machine.

'Hey, Meneer Chris, you here?'

It was six o'clock. The first milk cart rattled by on the street outside.

11

He heard Lottie cycle down the garden path, waited for the sound to die away, and decided to go inside. Not decided, really, he just went, almost without thinking. His life with Julia, with the factory, with his wife, it all ebbed and flowed in parallel with whatever he was thinking or doing, unobtrusively and as a matter of course.

He crossed the hall, left his hat on the ledge by the coat-stand, felt his way through the unlit sitting room, and opened the doors to the terrace. He could see the mist rising from the fen in the light from the bedroom window. Switched on by Van Dijk, as usual. Van Dijk, dependable minder of his daily existence.

Dudok pushed the wicker lounger further out onto the terrace and turned the outdoor heater on: two glowing bars radiating warmth. He took the rug from the back of the chair, wrapping it around him. Rolled up like a mummy, he stared into the night. Cigarette between his lips.

He inhaled the smoke, felt no effect. Should he write Lottie a note telling her how comforting her presence had been, and how touching the way she waved goodbye when she rode off on her bicycle? The thought dissolved the moment it arose. No point in foisting his sentiments on her. Give Stoetwegen a bell? Not a bad idea, even if it was half past one in the morning. Likely as not he would be hunched over his umpteenth whisky.

Stoetie, his friend from university, the hapless tippler. Never grew up, never shed his wayward fancies. Hot-headed little chap, like a perennial shadow at his side. Dudok had sheaves of letters from him, all written on an old typewriter with damaged keys, endless accounts of his life on Walcheren, the drinking parties, his lack of money and his flirtations. The eternal bachelor in search of romance, he frequently reported making a New Conquest. Five epistles on and she would be dismissed as a Write-Off.

Stoet's letters poured balm on Dudok's soul. They were what had kept him going in recent years, he would sometimes even wait for the postman to arrive. Walcheren, Domburg by the sea, it was all there in his mind's eye: the island's smart set crowded together in the bar of the Badpaviljoen with native son Stoetwegen at the centre, gesticulating and flailing his arms like a man

103

drowning. Which he was — in drink, with only his own jokes to keep him afloat. Of minor nobility was Stoet, worthy stock. But pedigree meant nothing to him, it was more of a hindrance than a help, as he saw it. He had visions of marrying a shop girl, a cashier he knew was ranked as a Stunner, the cloakroom attendant at the Badhotel as a Magnet-in-a-Dress, his landlady's housemaid as a Perfect Peach. Drink, a life of drink and disappointment, with not a hair's breadth of change for the better. Dudok had remained loyal to him throughout, before the war, during the war, and right up to the present. Wouldn't do to think too much about Stoetie, under the circumstances. It would only unleash old emotions, confused memories, pangs of remorse, even. But he forbore to stave them off.

It was late August, ten years after the war. Chris and his wife were lodged at the Hotel Britannia in Vlissingen, overlooking the boulevard and the new seaport. They were waiting for Stoetwegen, who would be coming over from Middelburg to meet them. He was late, and when he finally burst in he seemed more agitated than usual. His entrances were always somewhat flurried, but this time he was like a ship in heavy seas. Chris couldn't help laughing as he motioned him to calm down.

'What's up, Stoet? Another conquest?'

Stoetwegen glowered at them both, promptly ordered a glass of wine, began to say something, stopped, and mumbled an apology — had to get his breath back, terrible bus ride, standing room only.

Their days in Vlissingen had remained in his memory as luminous and clear — a miracle, really — and filled with a sense of extraordinary lightness, as though a long-standing burden of suspicion had suddenly been lifted from his shoulders. Chris seized every opportunity to wander about the harbour, where German vessels in growing numbers docked nowadays. The post-war decade had seen the full recovery of international trade, the factory was flourishing. Many of their machines were destined for Germany, the quiet, seldom-mentioned hinterland, despised business partner, inexorable and insatiable neighbour, stormbird of the new prosperity. Much had changed during that decade, many new avenues explored. Volkswagen cars were seen on Dutch roads, German was once again spoken at Zandvoort, Domburg welcomed the first coachloads of tourists from the east. Chris preferred doing business with France or Norway, but his technicians were just as happy being dispatched to Hamburg or

Frankfurt as to Oslo or Bordeaux. At Vlissingen, with the open sea just around the corner, you could observe the whole world steaming into port, more so than in Rotterdam. And you could vanish just as readily, out onto the open sea and into the world at large.

For years the three of them had been close. Stoet always turned up, wherever they went. Italy, the South of France, Zeeland. He spent weekends at their house, arriving and departing in a whirl of stories. Stoet had become the focus of their marriage, it seemed, a sort of indispensable link. Without him the emptiness became burdensome; he restored a measure of animation and drive to their life. The process had been gradual, Stoet himself would not even have noticed, given his shamelessly erratic ways and his permanent state of infatuation.

The day after Stoet's belated arrival they were to take a trip to Domburg, where the bathing season was drawing to a close. Chris, however, stayed behind: he was in no mood for crowded beaches, and glad for Stoet to go with his wife. He would be fine, books aplenty, new ships to check out, a stroll along the boulevard; no, no worries on his account, have fun, see you this evening.

They set off like children, his wife at the

wheel. Stoet, sitting beside her, wound the window down to cry *'Luctor, Chris, et emergo!'* The motto of Zeeland, and a stock phrase of his, often heard during weekends at their large house. He was inclined to hang around in the sitting room after Chris and his wife had retired, and his invariable response to their pleas not to stay up too late was a shout of *'luctor et emergo!'* Stoet was hard put to emerge.

Chris returned to the Britannia lobby with mixed feelings. The cheerful complicity in which they had driven off held no attraction for him, and yet there was something engaging about it. Should he go after them? He could take the bus, although it would take a while to get there. From Vlissingen to Domburg by bus, that would be a change. There was a stop on practically every corner in every village, where the driver would wait for people waving their walking sticks to come running from far off. World Record slow transport, and a hellish assault on one's patience. But why not surprise them? He could return with them by car, and there was no hurry.

By the time he boarded the bus the morning was as good as over. A seat at the front just behind the driver was free. This was the starting point of the expedition across the heartland of Walcheren. Koudekerke, Biggekerke, Meliskerke, Aagtekerke, villages enclosed by cornfields, maize crops, pastureland. God-fearing, churchgoing land by the look of it.

The bus stopped in Biggekerke. His thoughts turned to the poet who once lived there.

'Once more this life is strange, like waking up on a train in another country . . . '

The best description he had ever heard of the sensation he had almost every day: like waking up on a train in another country. Jolting awake, no idea where you are — what, travelling? Unfamiliar sounds, voices on the platform, a stationmaster's whistle, train pulling slowly away, pine forests, hills, mist outside the window.

Across Biggekerke, bumping along the cobbled high street, onward to Meliskerke. Bicycles on the road, farmers in the fields, haystacks, rippling corn — calendar pictures all.

He sat motionless in his window seat, absorbed in the landscape, lost in the poet's lines.

They were surely nearing their destination. Wasn't that the Westkappelle lighthouse on the far left, and the outskirts of Domburg rising up on the right? Long before the war he had been a regular visitor there, on family outings in his father's Pontiac, nanny on board, trunks in the boot, hampers on the roof. Not that he cared about any of that any more. His youth was a closed chapter as far as he was concerned; it seldom entered his mind apart from the odd detail, such as the make of a car, the name of a hotel, the number of his room, which was 224. He could not imagine the hotel having had so many rooms.

He got off the bus in the centre of the village, in bright sunshine. The high street was deserted, the shops were closed. Half-past one: everybody was at the beach, or else having lunch. The café terrace next to the town hall was empty but for a handful of people in desultory poses. He set off at a leisurely pace, in keeping with the siesta hour, towards the Badhotel, the haunt of the rich and privileged for the past century. They would be taking tea there later, he expected. The lawn in front of the hotel had various seating arrangements with parasols, mostly unoccupied. He walked on, through the park with its attractive cottages on either side, meaning to strike across the dunes to the lane leading to Carmen Silva, the house belonging to Stoet's friends. He was sure he would find his wife there, Stoet had planned their assignation that very morning. He saw no-one, and took the path through the copse of holm oak. Not a soul. Lovers' Lane, a hollow track with a canopy of green, thickets of bramble left and right, rampant ivy, not a speck of sunlight. The architect of this secret pathway to the shore could not be other than the sea breeze.

Rounding a bend, he saw them some way ahead, hand-in-hand, her head tilted to his shoulder. They were walking very slowly, even stopping now and then. He felt deeply moved, to his surprise. Then Stoet took her in his arms. Their kiss lasted an eternity. Chris watched, fascinated. Never had he seen her like that, never had he embraced her like that, not with such passion.

Stoet and his wife moved on, out of the leafy tunnel into the blazing sunshine, while he remained lurking in the dark-green shade. Even if they looked back they would not spot him. He let them go, theirs was the lingering pace of love. Or was it despair that bound them?

Something between the two, then, something halfway between abandon and default, he concluded later. Why had he felt that surge of relief, why no shadow of anger, not the slightest sense of betrayal or rupture? Quite the opposite, in fact: he had not wished to disturb them in any way, had merely followed them with his eyes as they vanished into the

110

dunes on their way to Carmen Silva. He would allow them time to collect themselves before confronting Stoet's friends. Chris sat down to wait on a dune not far from the water tower which stood precariously close to the shore, he thought. Still, the stone structure did not look out of place, it provided a pleasing counterpoint to the scrubby landscape, a vast no-man's-land stretching all the way round to Roomput and Vrouwenpolder, even possibly as far as Veere.

The sound of the gulls and the sea took him back to Travemünde. The sense of relief must have come from there. It no longer fell to him alone to love and cherish his wife. His commitment to her had been half-hearted for some time already, and this way he felt less guilty towards her for not giving Julia up. Or rather, he *had* given her up, by making himself scarce, regardless of having done so at her behest.

'You must promise me that you'll leave today, or you'll be putting me at risk.'

Her last trump card: you'll put me at risk if you stay. Pathos of the moment, or was the danger real? Why had he listened to her, why had he obeyed her so meekly? That question had never left his mind. The answers he fabricated for himself were many and varied, but none of them satisfied.

For months after his premature return he fought his desire to take the train back to Lübeck. The factory had fenced him in with endless duties. His father had retired, Chris had been handed the keys. And then the final straw: his father had died, as he had predicted in his letters. So much for all the advice he had stored up for his son. How to keep going during the war, how to obtain orders — it had all been a question of improvisation. Not that his father would have had a foolproof recipe. His father had fallen off his bicycle and dropped dead. Heart failure. He had never taken much of an interest in his father, had never really talked to him, or indeed listened. Decades in each other's company, same goal, same enterprise, same concerns, but apart from that they were opposites, barely recognizable as father and son. He had not grieved unduly, although the way his father was found had been distressing. Pinned under his bicycle, his coat torn and a gash on his forehead. Going to all that trouble in search of food, pedalling for half a day, and then to die like that.

Chris sat on his dune-top. Stoet and his wife were nowhere in sight. The water tower with its brass bowler hat to the left, to the right a house named Little Haven, shutters closed, all apparently tranquil in the sunshine. Not a soul, nobody to sit beside him and point to people on the shore.

'Look, Chris, guess what they're making down there!'

Just below them on the beach at Travemünde there had been an entire family building a miniature town in the sand, complete with approach roads marked by small flags, twigs and shells, and a sign on a big piece of paper saying 'Berlin, Unter den Linden'. Julia read the notice aloud, facing him, her legs dangling over the edge of the rocky platform, her toes not quite touching the sand. In the distance behind them lay the Café-Restaurant Seetempel, where Chris had kissed her hand, where she had answered his look, his questions, where she had seen the longing in his eyes.

'That's where they're rounding up Jewish people, and plundering their homes. Suicide is the order of the day, it's their last resort. Unter den Linden, Chris, is a main street of robbery and murder and persecution. That family playing so nicely in the sand are actually playing with fire. How nice to get their kids to build a model of Berlin, but how naïve. Criminally naïve. Unter den Linden sounds appealing, doesn't it? Like a painting of a summer afternoon, it would be enough to send you to sleep. That same avenue snakes through the dreams of the Jews, through their desperate, unsustainable dreams. They're being rounded up, Chris, the lot of them. They have all got to go. You don't know a fraction of what's going on. Things are only just beginning to happen in Lübeck and Travemünde. Come back here in a year or two and you'll see — except there's no way they're going to let you into the country by then.'

For the umpteenth time he wondered who Julia was, how she knew all these things, where she was staying, who her friends were.

'I used to walk down Unter den Linden so often, Chris. Andreas and I had our favourite café there, the Danzig. It had a small open-air terrace where we used to meet with a bunch of friends, often staying until two in the morning. Idealists, all of them, rebels, actors, musicians, future lawyers, aspiring architects and engineers, the so-called scum of the nation. We would quote Karl Kraus and say: 'Germany used to be the land of poets and thinkers, *Dichter und Denker*, but now it's all *Richter und Henker*, judges and hangmen.' We saw them all coming, the S.A. boys with their flags and their songs and their violence. Unter den Linden changed colour, it gradually turned brown and black. I was living near the Alexanderplatz at the time, a

114

five-minute walk from the university. Then in 1933 Andreas and I moved to Zehlendorf, well away from all those maniacs. There were woods there, and yet we were still in Berlin. We were very poor, having just finished our studies, but we found a flat in the Parrot neighbourhood, in a crescent of differently coloured houses. Andreas made friends wherever he went. He didn't care about prestige or social status, Jewish not Jewish, it was all the same to him. He badly wanted a part in a film, and Babelsberg, our own Hollywood, was nearby. But it soon became obvious that you didn't get very far unless you had connections in the regime. And we didn't have any. I found a job in an engineers' office dealing exclusively with projects relating to the Olympic Games. Oh, those wretched interlocking Olympic rings, I couldn't stand the sight of them after a while, they were everywhere: on the letterheads, on every invoice, on every desk, enough to drive anyone mad. And yet, looking back, those two years in Zehlendorf were incredibly carefree. Things were still open then. Andreas joined his first theatre company, I designed my first bridge. A bridge, Chris, the ultimate wish of every engineer. The miracle of the bridge, the triumph of calculation. The engineer's dream come true.'

'And your bridge — was it built? Did you manage to walk over it?' Chris did not face her as he said this, he was staring at the sand formations presided over by the proud family.

'I think it was built, but I had already been sacked before I had a chance to try it out.'

'Why did you lose your job, Julia, what went wrong?'

'Wrong? I was quicker than most of my male colleagues, perhaps that was my trouble. I don't think I did anything wrong, really. But I didn't join in with them, and they couldn't place me; besides, I was living with my brother who was an actor with the wrong kind of friends. I don't know, they just sacked me, I never discovered the exact reason. From then, on everything changed. Those two years in Zehlendorf seemed fresh as the morning dew, happy years, at least that's what I like to think. With hindsight it seems incredible how happy-go-lucky we were. Andreas came home every night exhausted but glowing, he was acting, he got applause, he had success. His first proper role with a proper theatre company, Chris, it was sensational! He had worked so hard to achieve that, it was his lifelong ambition. If only Father and Mother could have seen him.'

Julia paused. Chris noticed that she did not say 'parents', but 'Father and Mother'. He

116

was touched by the connotation of intimacy.

'I never missed them as much as on the first night of Andreas' first play. He was constantly on stage in those years, like a man possessed. He knew there were rough times ahead for the theatre. Bertolt Brecht had already fled, Walter Hasenclever was in France, Franz Werfel was living in Vienna and had virtually stopped writing. But there was still the classical repertoire of non-political tragedies and comedies. Andreas did them all. The piece you saw was a translation of a Danish classic, set in another time. So no risk there, you'd think. It was the premiere. Of course I knew he was playing the leading role with a small cast, and that he directed the play himself. What he did at the end must have been sheer impulse. He hadn't reckoned with the man in black in the front row. We told each other everything, even when we were back in Lübeck and not sharing the same apartment anymore.'

Chris had a strong sense that she was less forthcoming with him. For one thing, she did not mention her friends, nor those of her brother. He understood, and did not press her.

So she had been happy for two years of her life, he thought, just two. And he, had he known happiness, if only for two years?

117

Could he say with certainty that he had been happy at any particular time? Happiness was such a vague concept. It had never been something he consciously sought; in fact the word was almost embarrassing to him. He was unfit for it, unequipped, unwilling even to think in such terms.

Those moments in her company, the evening in the Grand-Café, the mornings at Lube-cawerke with her at her drawing board, that afternoon at the beach, that interminable, irreversible afternoon. Years hence it would be those moments, that time, that would count as the happiest he had known. Taken all together, what did they add up to? A few days, a fortnight?

Domburg in the early afternoon. Hunkered down on his sun-scorched dune, Chris was hard put to extricate himself from his memories. Now and then a rabbit flashed past. Seagulls went in pursuit of a large black crow, invader of their airspace. His eyes registered the spectacle, but he could not relate to what he saw. And had seen.

Stoet and his wife would have reached Carmen Silva by now, they would be sipping white wine on the terrace overlooking the lane along the beach. How would they react if they saw him arriving from the same direction? No, of course that wouldn't do at all, he would turn around and go back to the hotel, save them embarrassment. He stood up and retraced his steps, now in a hurry, afraid he might yet cross them in the village. The high street was even sleepier than before. He was just in time for the bus. It was slowly pulling away, but stopped again equally slowly to let him on when he waved his hat at the driver.

'Ah, so the lady didn't show, then?' he grinned. Chris returned the grin: it was the same driver as before.

'No, I was too late.'

A repeat of the previous journey: the villages, the poet, the cornfields. His wife and Stoet — it was curiously comforting to think he no longer owed her exclusive attention.

Chris was on his return journey, but for how long?

12

Not for much longer. The night wore on, the temperature dropped, and a gentle breeze began to blow at last. He did not feel cold under his rug, rather, he felt slightly feverish. Not coming down with something, was he? How bizarre to be concerned about a thing like that. Sheer habit.

He wondered how his brother would take the news of his death. No doubt he would bang down the receiver in a fury, jump into his car and dash over here to lambaste Van Dijk for not keeping a closer eye on his employer. Flying into a rage to mask his grief. His younger brother was irascible, but loyal to the core. Chris had taken him on at the factory after his stint in the Indies, where he had seen action. He had returned disillusioned and broken. Chris had gone to Hook of Holland to meet him at the docks. My God, the faces of those soldiers. Etched into his memory, they were. A year in the *dessas* of Java, the colonial territories exploited by their fathers and forefathers, the land of Multatuli and Couperus, the land of antiquated dreams. They had laughed alright, but not out

120

of fun, they had cried, but not with tears of normal sorrow.

He drove his brother home in the car, having dispensed with his chauffeur for the occasion. It was raining, the windscreen wipers swished together and away with reassuring rhythm. They spoke little.

He seldom called his brother by his name, always 'bro' or 'matey' or 'laddie', diminutives to express familiarity and affection. Not so on this occasion.

'Tell me, Coen, what was it like out there? It didn't sound too bad in your letters, but that's not the impression I got when I saw you all coming ashore.'

Coen did not reply. His military uniform made him look older than his age. He was twenty-four, a late-born son, but not too late to be roped in for the protection of Dutch interests overseas. 1950, and the Netherlands East Indies were no more. Now and then a car came from the opposite direction. The empty road, the chugging motor, the sound of wet tyres, the windscreen wipers, and the mute landscape all around. The blank inscrutability of it all.

Coen's lack of response to the question and the answer Chris had supplied instead said enough. What was it like out there? A hopeless, scandalous mess. A disgrace beyond description, a filthy little war. Chopping knives and coconut trees, and a whole lot more. Coen would not unburden himself, he would keep his mouth shut, that was the only fitting answer to an insane question. *Dessa*, the word stuck in his craw. The East Indies, or Indonesia for that matter, made him sick. His hot temper had not cooled.

Chris pulled up at their family home, standing empty now as their mother, too, had died fairly soon after the war. A quiet woman, married to a quiet man. Birth, marriage, life, death, the briefest of short stories. Of her three children Coen had been the closest to his parents.

'Come and join us at the factory, Coen. You'll have to take my place eventually, so this is as good a time to start as any.'

Echoes of his father's letter to him, echoes of his burning desire to give it all up as soon as his brother could take over. He had been running the company for over a decade, all those years since the letter dropped through his letterbox in Lübeck, all those years of unrelenting pressure. And the end was not in sight.

Coen stared at him as though he could hear gunfire far off, as though he had driven into an ambush, snarled jeeps, low-range gunfire, damn, back, turn back, get reinforcements. His service cap was tucked under the strap on his shoulder — he had remained a sergeant, eschewing the higher ranks.

'Not yet, Chris, not just yet.'

Driving away, he glanced in his rear-view mirror and saw Coen standing by the front door. He had insisted on being dropped off, not accompanied inside. He just stood there, luggage at his feet, motionless, as though nailed to the spot.

The rug kept slipping down. Dudok pulled it up again automatically, for fear of catching cold. He had a horror of draughts, as a result of which he favoured wearing a scarf at all times. Habits and gestures maintained to the end. Routine is stronger than death.

Of course Coen had joined the factory, of course he had eventually taken over the management. Dear old bro, ever unlucky in love, with a wife who turned to drink. Chris had warned him against the woman, but had not reckoned with Coen's drive, or with the serviceman's dedication. The factory became his wife, his companion on his journeys to countries where their machines were being installed. He roamed the world in the name of the client, in the name of his family, of his workforce.

Chris loved his brother. Loved him and envied him the freedom regained after his divorce. Laddie, soldier, ever upstanding, whatever the odds.

'Why go to the bloody Indies, for crying out loud! We have no business being there. We already got what we wanted, whatever it was. Take one look at the Van Stolkweg in The Hague and you can see what I mean: all those showy mansions, and not only there but all over. Read Du Perron or Multatuli and you won't want to go near the Indies. For whom, for what?'

His cynicism had got the better of him. Chris would try to dissuade his brother from his ill-conceived intent. But Coen wanted to fight. He had been too young for the Grebbeberg battle and too young to join the Resistance, much to his dismay in the post-war years. Now it was his turn. Tough work, preferably, with a gun on his shoulder, or manning a cannon or a howitzer or whatever they were called. Artillery, just the ticket. His own man at last, his own course of action. Sergeant Major Coen Dudok reports for duty.

It was all a fiasco, a sorry mess of murder, rape, desertion; not a shred remained of Coen's initial enthusiasm. The horrors he lived through would be locked away for the rest of his life. He shunned the veterans' reunions, refused to read about the conflict unless it was written by someone who had witnessed the events. Events, sorties into the jungle, punitive strikes on villages, vengeance and reprisal, and no ground gained whatsoever.

Only once did Chris get him to open up. It was at their club in town where the members gathered after work, with a bowling alley, a reading table and a bar. They had left the factory together before it closed and the club was still deserted, with the barman idly rinsing glasses that were already clean. A beam of sunlight fell across the large conference table.

Fifteen years at least had passed since Coen's return from Indonesia. Chris felt the time drawing near that he could step down as head of the company in favour of his brother. They were in accord about that, there were no obstacles, Coen was prepared.

Chris pointed to the group portrait taking up half the opposite wall; it was impossible to overlook.

'There. Father — at exactly the same age as you are now, bro.'

The notables of the town stared back at them, their father standing just left of centre, earnest, immaculate, unfathomable, in possession of a son for some time.

'Did you know that I missed him every single day, over in Java?'

Chris held his glass to his lips, but quickly set it down again.

'That bad, was it?'

'Worse, Chris, it beggars belief. I won't bore you with the nightmares I suffer as a result, but I have learnt to live with them. I've always been grateful that you got me involved in the factory so early on. I don't know what I'd have done otherwise.'

'Why did you miss him so? I don't believe I missed him much myself. He was not very communicative, and I took that as a sign of disapproval.'

'He was far more important to me than I ever realized when he was alive. A cliché, I know, but it happens to be true. I got to know him very well during the war, Chris. You were married by then, but I was living at home. Whenever there was an air raid he stood by me, and by Mother, like a sheepdog, quiet and watchful, all concentration. I was devastated when he died. They brought his bike back, with his broken glasses and his torn coat; they even brought the sack of food he'd bought from the farmer. I was seventeen, Chris, and there was no way for me to express my grief. Later on, in Java, I missed him with a vengeance. Broken bikes, smashed glasses, ripped jackets: I saw them everywhere, and each time I saw Father. And

126

with each manoeuvre I thought of him, the way he stood in the living room or in the hallway, like a sentry, a gatekeeper, his eyes fixed on us, alert. He was there for us.'

Chris had kept silent, not wishing to disturb his brother in his report from that unknown front. Then the members began to arrive, and Java and their father faded away. Loud greetings, the bowling alley came alive, the barman was run off his feet.

In the soft, monotonous buzz of the terrace heating, Chris Dudok drifted in and out of sleep. At the factory, in his office, he used to hear the similar buzz of distant machines, a continuous twittering sound, Morse signals from the production area. The administration section was worlds apart from the dirty hands, the metal shavings, the pounding pistons of the great lathe. But he was often to be seen on the shop floor among the machines, he knew everybody, chatted with newcomers, never went home without first having spoken with the warehouseman. He had developed a routine so fixed that his workforce could set their watches by his arrival in their midst. Meneer Chris, in his signature three-piece suit, regardless of weather or season. In winter he would more often than not wear a trilby, and very rarely ventured forth without a waist-coat, even in a heatwave. He had shackled himself to convention, to strict decorum in dress, manners and language, so as not to lose himself in the freedom he had once tasted. It was the carapace of his displacement.

In the course of time he seemed to have put an increasing distance between himself and the men on the shop floor. It had not been his intention. The change was not due to the men, it was he who had changed. Many of them had witnessed the factory's renaissance back in '45: a job at Dudok's was one for the long term. Forty, even fifty years of service were not unusual. Such occasions merited an address, which he would deliver out of habit. But with increasing brevity, terseness, detachment.

His speech on the return of the *Heyligens-taedt* had made a deep impression. He had never spoken with such resonance again, the glow of that single occasion had never returned. His bravura had not even lasted the night, indeed, it had left him disconsolate.

His wife had been so excited that day, her hopes of a child rekindled. Dudok's child, an impossibility. The merits of fatherhood that were quietly being propagated all around him left him indifferent. From father to son, he had heard it often enough; a conservative dream. From father to son, creating a livelihood and wishing to pass it on to the next generation, whether they want it or not. From father to son, to son, to son.

Dudok's love for his grandfather went much deeper than for his father. Love sometimes skips a generation. He could hear the disappointment and even vexation in his grandfather's voice asking what on earth he expected to find 'over there'.

'Over there' was the other side of life, the wrong side. 'Over there' was the factory and un-freedom, 'over there' was the son who had gone against his father's wishes and struck out on his own, thereby renouncing all that had been so carefully nurtured and made to prosper.

There they all were, in the hour of Dudok's dying deed. He had not summoned them; they appeared of their own accord. Of these visitors it was perhaps his grandfather who was the most anchored, he who had been master of untold meadows, corn crops, hayfields. The setting of his boyhood holidays. School meant going back home, it meant a remote bogeyman keeping him away from his grandfather, away from a kingdom of apple trees and stables and the licking tongues of young cattle. His hand being sucked by the toothless maw of a calf, a tingling sensation, anticipation of a woman in his embrace. His fingers being licked as he dangled them over the gate, bright sunshine, flies, the smell of manure, the sense of not being watched, the sense of freedom.

The farm was called De Bredelaar; the name suddenly revealed itself with icy clarity. It reminded him of the wingspan of an eagle. The name was lodged in the depths of his soul. A house to die in, fields to be inherited, properties to be cherished. It was not to be. The grandfather had lost his son to the city, to a space filled with metal and machines. And his grandson had been lost from the beginning, as the old man saw it — rightly so, Chris thought. He knew all about the feeling of banishment, awayness, not belonging. It was something he had made every effort to avoid. But deep within him was the funnel, the empty vessel, the future fall.

13

In the hours of his dying deed, they all came by. Of their own accord, uninvited, unforgiving. Grandfather, Coen, Stoet, and his wife, whose name he had hidden away, to be uttered sparingly, if ever. She had several nicknames, but even those he avoided. She called him Chris, later Dudok, occasionally Dude, but those monikers were likewise seldom heard in their house.

Upon his return from Germany, of which he never spoke, she had been the first to come forward. She lived nearby, and was already in the starting blocks. A jolly girl, not without her attractive moments, and raring for opportunity. She set about casting her net with slow deliberation. He was no longer the man she had waved goodbye to back in '37. Outwardly the same, and no less charming in her eyes, but she was unsure how to approach him, given the rise in his natural reserve. It only made her more cautious and wary in her scheming.

She had suggested they take a day off together. Late March, bright sunshine, just enough wind to go sailing. They had gone to

Reeuwijk, where the boat club was more or less deserted. He had been tied up with the factory for months, in closer contact with his father than ever before. He often found himself fighting the urge to drop everything and walk away. Away, back. But the pressure from the family business, combined with his father's tenacity and the Dutch girl's attentions were wearing him down. The dearth of news from Germany worsened his doubts as to Julia's feelings for him. Her silence deafened him. Little by little his winter and summer in Lübeck were smothered away, along with the autumn, and the month of November.

Very well, then, he would take the day off, sit back and let things happen.

She came to collect him in her car; all that was required of him was to get in beside her. The weather was exceptionally mild, close on twenty degrees. She began to sing, not too badly either, he thought. And she was a better driver than he was. He was won over by her unfailing good humour. Go sailing? Madness. Neither of them knew how to sail. A rowing boat, now that he could manage, but all that rigmarole with sails, ropes and fenders — not quite his idea of fun.

She was aware of that. She parked at the club house, took a picnic basket from the back seat and led the way. Purposefully, even brazenly, all caution thrown to the wind, so it appeared. He trailed after her. The bright sunshine made up for a lot, and he was curious to see what she had in mind. Thank God, a motor-boat. Mannus the boatman stood by, glad for something to do.

'A perfect day, sir. Your good lady is ready for the fray, I see.'

They stepped on board, laughing.

Your good lady?

They manoeuvred their craft away from the wooden jetty, past several sailing boats whose owners were either busy with tar brushes or scrubbing decks. Chris gave her a sidelong look. He had to admit that it had not been a bad idea of hers to go out on the lakes. They set off, out of the small marina, and gathered speed. She donned a cap, blue with a white peak, the ultimate yachting cap.

'Graciously loaned by Mannus, who bought it for his daughter,' she told him happily, as she opened the throttle.

She was at the helm, finally steering in the direction of her choosing. She craved speed, and she craved his attention. The first fine morning of the boating season, the first sails on the horizon. Blue herons, moorhens, scattered islets of reeds and grass. Reeuwijk, an expanse of marshland, sunken meadows, a maze of channels, you could never tell quite where you were, let alone navigate.

She had no fixed course. Just letting the engine putter on and having him standing or sitting close by was all she wished for. Four months had passed since his return, four months of hard graft at the factory. Chris had a keen sense of what was going through her mind. She saw his expression change, and feared he was drifting away from her. The man who had fascinated her for years, who held her at a remove, who ignored her and led her on by turns depending on his mood: he was the one she had set her heart on. She would make him her husband, whatever it took.

Whatever?

'See that island, Chris? Let's go and have our picnic there. We can easily tie up at the little landing stage.'

'You should come and work with us at the factory, we can always do with an enterprising spirit.'

'Ah, in that case, may I apply for a job with you?'

She touched his arm fleetingly. He did not reply, refused to think, felt himself being driven to a conclusion.

'Careful, Chris, hold off with the boat-hook, or we'll crash into the side.'

'Steady on, steady on. Put her into reverse then I'll manage the hook just fine.'

'I say, boss, I think we make a pretty good team, don't you?'

Chris Dudok, company director, thirty-one years of age, single — as yet — stepped ashore. He tipped an imaginary hat, took her hand to help her out of the boat, and did not release it until they had crossed the landing stage. She looked at him, tucked some loose strands of hair under her cap, and led him to a patch of grass alongside the boat. He observed the glow on her face, felt the fire in her body. He had held her hand for the length of a landing stage: his way of acknowledging his return. He had so often ignored her these last months, he had been uncaring towards her, treated her like a stranger. So this was presumably the start of something new. Easy now, keep quiet, shield your eyes, ignore your blood, forget her hand and her nearness. Don't look back, let it all go, abandon the boat and everything else. Go for it.

Chris said nothing, neither did she.

A quiet Friday morning brimming with questions. He imagined finding himself in the middle of an answer one day, by surprise. Unwittingly, unwillingly spending the rest of his life with her, the woman beside him with her thermos, rug, handbag, and future within

135

reach. A sun-drenched isle, a place to have coffee. A tree trunk to sit on, a mug held aloft for her to replenish, steam curling round their mouths. Call it a springboard, a fork in the road, a costly moment of advance or retreat, of now or never. Which subjects were best avoided? Chris watched as she busied herself in her open-air kitchen, slicing the cake, laying the table.

'Picnic time, Chris. It'll be a change from coffee at the factory.'

He gave a little bow, tapped her on the shoulder, invited her to take a seat and ceremoniously adjusted her tree-trunk chair. The stage-set of their lives in later years: each on an island with much fresh air and cake. And much unspoken.

The coffee mood was prolonged until late in the day, and for years after. It was there, on that little island in the waters of Reeuwijk, that she achieved her victory. Or met her Waterloo. Or both. With hindsight you can say anything — that the motor-boat entered the wrong channel, for instance. The island was shaped like a comma, he noticed as they were leaving, and proceeded to tell her so.

'See that? Our island looks like a comma, so the story is not over yet.'

'Or like a question mark, Chris, or an ear. I'd say it's a story to be continued.'

Their symbolic accord made them laugh. On that day he found her more attractive, sweeter than before. She had kept a certain reserve — that had done the trick. Intimacy at arm's length, seduction by stealth, she was expert at both. They headed back in the same cheerful spirit as they had set out. Mannus caught the line they threw, enquired how they had fared and whether they had spotted the golden plover. Hardly likely, he supposed, did they even know what it looked like? Rain was in the offing, so they had returned in good time. The last sailing boats were tying up, the air was filled with the sound of canvas dragging over the gangways.

14

The stars above Dudok's reclining chair began to fade. The sky grew pale with the approach of dawn, chill and overcast.

Suddenly he felt shivery, from the cold, or a light fever, or was he just fearful and overwrought? No, not fear anymore, nor tension or despair. A surge of uncontrollable shaking erupted from deep within him, causing his chest to heave and his limbs to spasm. He pushed the rug away, took a sip of water and tried to calm himself. Without success: the trepidation persisted, his body resembling a seismograph of what was in store. He looked down at himself, the quaking legs, the twitching shoulders, the hands gripping the arm rests. A tidal wave, ship forging into dangerous waters, perilous reef, sand grating on the keel, nobody on deck, no help for miles around. The span of sky stood taut, soundless, a depopulated universe looming over the terrace.

Being powerless to stop his limbs from shaking was intolerable. Until then he had been fully in control of his plan, his mind at rest and free of all doubt. Van Dijk had dropped him off without suspecting anything, and he had walked the rest of the way, or rather shuffled like a blind man, until his rescue by the girl next door. Soon her parents would be waking her up. Had he switched the lights off? Had he locked the front door? The tremors began to subside, first in his legs, as though the storm in his blood had abated, then in his chest, and lastly in his arms. He felt a flood of relief, as if he had just had the narrowest of escapes. Bemused by this, he resumed waiting for the dawn.

My God, the pressure he had been under during that year. Boat trips, dinner parties, dances, she took him everywhere, inveigling him into her unflagging optimism. Yet he knew that she despaired of him at times. He had so often held back, pleading a heavy workload at the factory. There was the war of attrition with his father, with not a day going by without initiation into one or other secret of the profession. Profession? To him running a factory was not a profession, it was a *fait accompli*, a terrifying obligation, quite alien to his nature. His degree in economics had proved utterly useless, his entire education repelled him and stood in his way.

The first time he found himself in the office without his father had been extraordinary. He was most aware of the clock ticking, an old-fashioned timepiece with a dull tune marking each half hour. His day had passed in half-hours, the desk bare, silence outside the door, reading the newspaper, riffling through recent orders. He had felt an urge to visit the design department, but checked himself. Not until late afternoon, with the tea things cleared away by the secretary, did his father turn up. Likely as not he had spent a similar day waiting and watching the clock until he felt he could decently make his way to the works.

'Hello there, Chris! And how was your day?'

Pale and distracted, seated at the very desk his father had occupied for thirty years, the son who would live by the wind, who would read and travel, was unnerved by his father finding him there.

One day, when his father came to pick him up from his grandfather's at De Bredelaar, he had gone missing. He knew the story, it was one which his father had told him in a rare confidential mood. He had been quite young, ten or eleven maybe. The barns and the stables, the big orchard, the fields stretching to the horizon — his father said he had been impressed each and every time he went there. Young Chris was nowhere to be found, he had been gone since morning, because he knew he was being fetched that day. He could recall almost verbatim his father's words describing how he had finally found him. Lying in a field with his cheek against the flank of a calf, his hair standing up in the wind. The calf was dead, the glazed eyes were crawling with flies. He had stood there looking down at his son's ashen face, which bore no sign of any pleasure at being found by his father, just a blank stare. Chris had looked so defenceless lying on the ground beside the calf.

'It fell over, Father, and couldn't get up again.'

That was all he had said. He had got up and followed his father, more quietly than ever, as though he were scarcely there.

1939, the year he got married. In spite of himself. Holland was mobilizing her troops, the factory was running at full capacity, orders from Britain and Germany were pouring in. The race had begun, even milk powder machines were considered expedient. That time it had been Chris who suggested the Reeuwijk lakes. Same little boat, same island, same warm summer weather as a few months before. He held her hand again as they crossed the landing-stage, but when they reached their picnic spot he did not let go. He asked if she minded. He meant for now, or for as long as she wanted, or anyway for a fair number of years, in other words, for a lifetime. He believed he had reached a point in his life, or rather he would be very pleased, well, how should he put it — would she consider marrying him?

Even she must have been surprised to hear such a faltering, circuitous declaration of love. Was it a declaration of love? More like phrases hovering between need and doubt, stumbling in their haste to redress previous infelicities, like climbing a mountain, secured with ropes on all sides, struggling up and up and word for word to the summit and clear sky. But the leaden drawback remained unspoken. It was something he could not decently keep silent about, but neither could he bring himself to tell her.

Summer on the lake with sailing dinghies and paddle boats all around, light aircraft flying across the sky. Mobilization on all fronts. Soldiers rowing past, training for an army bound for defeat.

They sat together on their small island, in a haze between joy and sorrow. Because he had eventually told her. On no account would he become a father. There were to be no children. They heard the plaintive cry of grebes over the water, the splash of a jumping fish. He had looked away as he delivered his

142

verdict of ineptitude, but his tone had been one of unconditional resolve.

She did not ask why, she did not want to know when he had made that decision, she had no questions. She said nothing, did not respond, endured the words with difficulty.

Chris, too, was overcome, he could barely think how to proceed, could not recall what she had said before. Had she said yes? Had she accepted?

She took his hand, stared at it, stroked it briefly. And held on.

A seaplane landed near the army boats. They watched as a rubber dinghy was blown up and two men fled with the others in hot pursuit. War games. If marriage was their plan they had better not leave it too late.

He walked into it with his eyes open. She kept hers closed, dreaming that it would blow over. That one day there would be a child.

15

He stepped into the metallic world of the messe Frankfurt. Achema, the international trade fair for chemical engineering. A hall resembling a vast lighting emporium. A sea of machinery, apparatuses, glass spheres. It was thirteen years since the end of the war, sixteen years since the attack on — no, not that, away with it, don't think, banish from the record, stop, forget.

Chris set off in the direction of their stand in Hall 4. The Messe: he was back in the land of the enemy, back in the land of disillusionment and unconscionable loss. He had not been back since '38, not since his contemptible, crippling flight.

He had boarded his train to Frankfurt at the same station to which he had returned all those years ago, like a thief in broad daylight. He found himself crossing into Germany as furtively as he had departed, as though time had stood still, as though the war had never happened, the countryside immutable, devoid of any sign or indication of the evils of history, just a succession of houses, trees, hills, roads, a long cadence of harmlessness observed from a train window. Or so it appeared. The view bore down on him. Julia stood at every station; he saw her waiting at every level-crossing, riding bicycles, driving cars. Long cadence of the past, endless chain of impotence and guilt.

He had insisted on making the journey alone. His assistants had gone ahead, he would meet up with them at the Messe. In recent years the factory had resumed trade with Germany, his engineers and technicians had long since re-embraced the neighbours, but Chris himself had refused to go there. Traversing the Ruhr, full steam ahead to the new Wirtschaftswunder, he felt suffocated. It was the grim irony of history — reconstruction and modernization on a vast scale, all whistle-while-you-work, and all that money being poured into the heartland of German industry.

The terminus at Frankfurt took his breath away. Crowds of a size Chris had not seen for years, everything on a massive scale, orderly, cheerful. A throbbing din of progress, he could feel the city growing as he walked down the platform. It was a short ride by taxi to the fair; they dropped off his suitcase at the Hessischer Hof hotel on the way.

Reluctantly, he joined the stream of visitors pressing into the hall. The factory manufactured a wide range of products for the chemical industry, a field Chris was familiar with through trade fairs in Paris and London. But the most spectacular of these events was the Achema, with Germany as the self-proclaimed inventor of chemistry.

Before reaching the company stand he had already shaken a fair number of hands. French, Belgian, Italian. Thirteen years after the war and they were all go, all brightness and good cheer. Alert, resourceful, eager for trade, connections, new markets. A gigantic fairground without a past, a merry-go-round of mercantile minds. Paradise for the business agent, Valhalla for the engineer.

Chris advanced on feet of lead, as though sadness awaited him. His pace slackened further as he approached his people. He dreaded having to engage in conversations with clients he had never seen before, having to be polite, even friendly.

His diary for the coming days was filled with appointments, receptions, dinners. The Frankfurter Hof, the Schauspielhaus, his heart sank at the prospect. Why on earth had he agreed to the trip? He would never have done so had it not been for his brother. 'They' wanted to meet the head of the company, there would be three or four major contracts to sign, he really needed to be there in person. He should never have come; it was just that he thought he would be able to suppress his aversion, that he was free from it, free from the past.

Free?

The very idea. What a misconceived, bourgeois idea. How facile, how repugnant. Free — every schoolboy's dream, a free period, maths teacher on sick leave, no test to do. That was freedom, a dash into town, a golden opportunity lasting exactly one hour. The un-freedom he suffered from was of a different order. How to free yourself from the happiest months of your life? From memories of life-changing events, and of a parting that robbed you of your soul? How?

This was Julia's terrain. This hall was the kind of place where she belonged, even if she might never have actually been there — engineers as far as the eye could see. And why should she not be there now? Why should she not pop up all of a sudden, at one of the stands, chatting with colleagues? Why not indeed?

Dreamer, fantasist, self-deluder, get a grip. Rise to the occasion, shoulder your way through the crowd, force yourself to look and listen.

'Chris, we're over here! Good to see you!'

He had found his destination in the maze of aisles. The array of machines and familiar

147

faces brought him down to earth. He would do what was expected of him: make conversation, welcome visitors, promote, entertain.

The day passed in good order. Chris had no time for reflection of any kind. The din of the fair pulsed and boomed in his head. By the end of the afternoon, when the crowd began to thin, he felt as though he were recovering from general anaesthesia. It would soon be closing time, people were heading off to hotels and bars for drinks.

He sat nursing a cup of tea at a small table in their stand. Behind him stood his brother, deep in conversation with a colleague. He heard figures, names of clients, technical details of a new type of machine, but he was not listening. Lulled by their voices, he gazed at the technological panorama stretching out on all sides. The image dissolved into a great sprawling engine running idle, in patient abeyance of acceleration. Someone came strolling up the aisle towards him, slowly entering his field of vision. His hand lifting the tea cup froze in mid-air, his mouth forgot to drink, his ears throbbed with blood. He knew that man, there was something familiar about his bearing, but no, no, it couldn't be true, he was surely mistaken. Knollenberg. It had to be him.

It was indeed Knollenberg. Decidedly

older-looking, greyer, and heavier, but the pale, somewhat aloof expression was unchanged. Chris rose from his chair, considered taking flight, but stood where he was. Much as he wished to, he was unable to move.

Knollenberg drew ever nearer to the Dutch stand, apparently oblivious to the figure rising to his feet in greeting.

Then he halted, stiffening as he raised a hand to his balding pate.

'Herr Dudok?'

'Indeed I am, Herr Knollenberg. I saw you coming, how are you? It never occurred to me that we might run into each other. What a coincidence. I would love to invite you to step into our stand, but I'm afraid my brother and I have an appointment very shortly.'

Chris paused. Under no circumstances did he wish to enter into a conversation with Knollenberg within earshot of his younger brother.

'Perhaps we could arrange to meet later this evening?'

'Certainly, Herr Dudok, that would be a pleasure. But how are you? How very good to see you. So you pulled through alright?'

'I believe it should be me asking that question of you. Would ten o'clock suit you? In the lobby of the Hessischer Hof?'

Knollenberg gave a little bow, nodded in

149

confirmation of the time and place, and slowly moved away.

Chris sat down again. He twisted round to steal a glance at his brother, who was still chatting to his colleague. He felt a twinge of guilt, praying that Coen had not noticed the man. Knollenberg. How often, after the war, had he not considered making an effort to trace him. For no other reason than to discover whether he had any news of Julia. Knollenberg himself left him cold.

He had never got round to it, and besides, he did not need Knollenberg to tell him what had become of her. He did not need that man to tell him she was dead, murdered, done away with, whatever. Gone forever.

But her presence had never left him.

16

Hessischer hof, half past nine. Chris wanted to be sure he arrived before Knollenberg. There was a quiet corner with a settee, a low table and an armchair, where he sat down to wait. The bar just beyond was teeming with Messe visitors, noisily resuming contacts established earlier in the day. The volume of chatter rose with each fresh round of drinks. A heated atmosphere, with the promise of maudlin fraternization as the evening wore on. Chris resigned himself. He was still unable to think straight. His brain felt muffled. The encounter with the former head of Lubecawerke had thrown him completely off balance. Face to face with the man who had sent for him each morning and who had for close on a year briefed him on business matters. The man who had sacked Julia from one day to the next, although Chris seemed to remember him being none too happy about it.

Lubecawerke, Lübeck. Would it never end?

There had been a dinner to celebrate their new French contract, which he had left before the port was served. Smiles had been exchanged, hands shaken until a next time. He had waved absently to Coen: they would see each other in the morning. His brother was staying in a more centrally located hotel, along with the rest of the company staff. The Hessischer Hof, diagonally across from the Messe, catered for a rather grander clientele.

Climbing the broad steps to the entrance, he was seized with the same aversion as upon entering the fair that morning. Taxis came and went in the dark, the discreet lighting of the lobby windows forming a beacon in the murky street. He took up the *Frankfurter Allgemeine* only to lay it again aside; he had no interest in news of any kind. He waited.

He began to regret his impulsive invitation to Knollenberg. There could be no point to it. All those questions that would be asked, all those answers that he already knew, the awkward silences, the raising of glasses to renewed acquaintance, to the future, indeed, while they were about it, to Europe. Knollenberg was bound to have some spiel about how terrible it had been and how the German people had been betrayed and brutalized by the Nazis. Chris had heard it all before, but he had not forgotten how keen everybody was to join in, how Lubecawerke itself bristled with vigour and zeal.

The clock above the bar indicated ten. Just

then a waiter appeared at his table to take his order, so that he missed seeing Knollenberg arrive.

'Good evening Herr Dudok, I hope I did not keep you waiting,' he said, promptly turning to the waiter to add: 'The drinks are on me, Ernst.'

'Very well, Herr Knollenberg.'

'I happen to know Ernst, because I come here twice a week. I live in Frankfurt nowadays, we have meetings in this hotel.'

Knollenberg's self-assurance was undiminished. His even tone and decisive air did not portend an apologetic stance. He had aged, naturally, but he also seemed more open, friendlier even.

'I am delighted to see you, Herr Dudok. You were often in my thoughts.'

Chris was overwhelmed by Knollenberg's opening gambit. What reason could this German have had to think of him?

'Julia often spoke of you.'

At that moment Ernst set their drinks on the table, obscuring Knollenberg's face with his white mess-jacket sleeve.

What had he just said? That Julia had often spoken of him? She and Knollenberg on speaking terms? But it was Knollenberg who had kicked her out, he had even warned him against her.

153

'Better not associate with Fraulein Bender. She is no longer one of us.' The verdict given by Knollenberg all those years ago pounded in his brain.

Julia often spoke of you — had he heard correctly? It was beyond belief. The damning words 'she is no longer one of us' had blown him away, he had wanted to quit there and then. But his only hope of seeing Julia again was to stay in Lübeck, and for that he needed his job at Lubecawerke.

'One of us' — the perfidy of it. And who had he meant by 'us'? The rabble swarming in the streets of the city? All those torch-bearers, all those law-abiding citizens turning a blind eye, including Knollenberg and the rest of the management, all those engineers and architects, colleagues through thick and thin?

Talk of 'us' was a danger signal, there was always a 'them' hard by. A 'them' you could sack, or threaten, or report to the police.

Knollenberg and Julia had talked about him. Was Knollenberg making it up? Was he trying to ingratiate himself? Whatever the case, Chris was overwhelmed. He stared after the waiter as if he had seen a ghost, then shifted his gaze to his patiently expectant interlocutor.

'Are you saying that you were friendly with Julia Bender, the engineer you dismissed from her job?' His tone was unintentionally belligerent.

Knollenberg paled. His features assumed the old impenetrable expression Chris remembered so clearly.

'I was in contact with her for four years after that. I was able to be of help to her now and then. She stayed with me and my wife at our house a few times. We became good friends.'

Chris's bewilderment was palpable. Knollenberg was about to say something, but this time Chris interposed.

'Julia is dead, at least that is what I have always assumed, ever since the war.'

'Indeed, Herr Dudok, she did not survive the war. She was killed by a bomb during the attack on Lübeck at the end of March 1942.'

Of course he knew she was dead, it could not be otherwise, but to hear Knollenberg affirming the fact was excruciating. He made no comment, just as he had made no comment upon learning of Julia's dismissal that time at the office.

The liveliness in the lobby rose by leaps and bounds. A man threw his arms about a woman; there was a little burst of applause. From the hallway came the sound of violins.

'Don't look, Chris, carry on talking,' she had said when the gang of brownshirts spilled from the revolving door of Café Elzas. Julia Bender, dead. Julia Bender, killed by a British bomb. Julia Bender, whom he had abandoned to her fate.

'Let me explain, Herr Dudok. I realize what a shock this is to you. But I trust you will believe me when I say that it is still painful to me to speak of Julia, of her life on the run, of her pointless death.'

Knollenberg's tone was gentle and sincere. He enunciated Julia's name with such care and concentration that Chris believed him, wanted to believe him. He did not need to ask any questions, for Knollenberg began of his own accord. Chris listened intently, interrupting only a few times to ask after a specific detail or circumstance.

The scales had fallen from Knollenberg's eyes on the day of Julia's dismissal. That morning, the morning after the play, he had received a visit from the Gestapo, with orders to get rid of Fraulein Bender forthwith. Her brother was a Communist, second only to a Jew as a qualification of hatefulness.

He had protested that she was a first-rate draughtswoman and a hard worker, but they had taken no notice whatsoever.

'Let this be a warning,' was their well-rehearsed parting shot. In the language of the time it meant so much as: this is an order, carry it out at the double or you'll find yourself in Dachau or Buchenwald or some similar sunny home.

He had written the letter of dismissal by hand, not on the Lubecawerke stationery but on his own notepaper. No secretary had been involved; the contents of his letter were to remain private. He had taken a risk by asking the young Dutchman to deliver the envelope. And another risk by telling Julia the truth.

Yes, Knollenberg had indeed dismissed her, but under duress, as he explained in his letter. He had offered his assistance, had also given her the address of his brother in Weimar, who could be relied on to help if the need arose. Knollenberg's initiative was not without danger. How did he know she was not some sort of provocateur? He had given her the benefit of the doubt, could not conceive of her betraying him. And he had not been mistaken. On the contrary.

Knollenberg rambled on. About his rude awakening from the National Socialist dream, and how, once awake, his perception of reality had changed. During that summer of '38, when Chris frequented the seaside at Travemünde, he had met Julia on several occasions. That was when she was staying at her brother's place in the old town, but she had been away much of the time, travelling all over the country, lodging with friends, mostly in Berlin.

The police seemed to lose interest in her after a while, but Julia had remained on her guard. In the rule of arbitrariness an old, closed dossier could suddenly be dusted off and reopened.

She was not a Communist, far from it. She was independent-minded, ever astute in her assessment of the situation. She discussed these matters with him, and with numerous others, as far as he knew. Talking with her was like a breath of fresh air, especially in those dark days of wholesale distrust and censorship, when a normal exchange of ideas was all but impossible. With her, though, it was no holds barred. She was recklessly honest and outspoken.

She took her scalpel to the propaganda and the politics, dissected the German reign of terror, laid bare the impotence of the self-respecting bourgeoisie, the feebleness of the generals, the silence of the Church — although she knew of a few exceptions in that quarter. She also knew about tens of thousands of dissenters being held in a variety of prison camps. She could reel off all the names of the camps, where they were situated, on the outskirts of this town or that village, not far from this factory, in the neighbourhood of that forest. There had been Kristallnacht in November, of course, but in the previous summer she had already passed on news of broken-glass incidents in Berlin, Munich and Leipzig.

Merely possessing that kind of information could be fatal. How she obtained it he had never asked, but he trusted her implicitly. She had to be right, there was no doubt possible, he could see it wherever he turned.

She had spoken of Chris Dudok more and more often after Kristallnacht, when she spent a week at Knollenberg's house. She had told them she was glad Chris had got away, but had sounded very sad. It had been a very difficult time for her.

'You were her lover, Herr Dudok?' His tone made plain that he had no doubt of the answer.

Chris nodded, stunned by the directness of the question. Her lover? Was that what he had been? A few hours, a summer long, months of hope and overture. Lover? A radiant word. He would not have dared to use it. Knollenberg had no such scruples.

'Did you not write to her, or go looking for her? Were you unable to reach her? Had you not arranged some means of keeping contact?'

The roles seemed reversed, with Knollenberg asking the questions, almost accusingly, and Chris trying to respond. Of course he had wanted to see her again, how many times had he been on the point of jumping on the train back to Lübeck? But he had given her his promise. She had made him go, made him promise to stay away and under no circumstances to try to find her. She would find him, she had said. All he could do was wait for the insanity to end. He would bide his time, he had thought, it would all be over before long. A grave mistake.

Lover. The question to which he had no answer. If only Knollenberg knew how Julia had steered the course of his life, or rather, truncated it. There were times when he felt as though nothing had happened since, nothing at all.

How long had she been waiting on the doorstep before he returned at five in the morning? Where had she been? The way she had turned her cheek to his hand, with her head tilted to one side, her eyes closed, her lips kissed, in such complete surrender as if it had always been thus: lovers at dawn. The red glow of fire in the distance, muffled cries and lit windows in the street.

This was the night that would never be over, the summary manifesto of destruction signed by Der Führer.

Her sweet face in his hand. He led her

inside, they stood close together, he took off her coat, she locked him in her arms. Their love was like no other. No two people had ever embraced in this way. Touched to the quick, rapture-bound until daylight. Lover?

Innocent question posed in the language of the executioner, of the past, of lost hope and failure. Chris Dudok had no answer.

Noting Chris's mortification, Knollenberg paused uneasily before resuming his story — fragmentary, of necessity, snippets from Julia's life, little things he remembered about her, but steeped in admiration throughout. It sounded like a a piece of music, which moved him anew each time he played it.

Was Chris aware that she had saved two Jews from falling into the hands of the S.A. during Kristallnacht? An elderly couple, whom she had warned in the nick of time and taken to a safe place. Had she told him about her contacts with enemies of the regime all over the country? Had he ever met her friends from Berlin, who went on to shelter Jews and forge ration cards, who wrote and distributed illegal pamphlets?

A Communist after all? Had it not been Knollenberg who suggested as much? Chris remembered his astonishment at hearing the term used in connection with Julia. He had even felt a twinge of alarm. Not that he had ever noticed anything. As far as he knew Communists went in for ponderous theorizing. Not she. Nothing he had read about them could possibly apply to her. All of a sudden it came to him that Knollenberg had wanted to shield her, possibly from him as a foreigner. And that Knollenberg had tried to scare him off.

'As a matter of fact, Julia was staying at our house when she had that miscarriage, three months after you left.'

Knollenberg spoke with deliberation, as though he had written the sentence long beforehand, and was reciting from memory.

Waiters paced to and fro. A cluster of men at the bar, glasses in hand, launched into a ballad. Someone sat down at the piano to play the accompaniment to the final verse.

Don't look, Chris, don't look, just carry on talking.

His mantra, his secret formula when in danger of losing control.

This time it did not work. He could not carry on talking, and it was impossible not to look.

He stared, speechless, the statement hovering in the air between them like a dragonfly above a dark pool. All at once it was there, a string of words carefully formed and punctuated; you could hear the full stop at

162

the end. Irrevocable, like a statement made to the police. Say the words and you are stuck with them for life. No need of paraphrase, or translation, no further questions either. He could see the sentence before him.

'Didn't you know, Herr Dudok?' Knollenberg asked in disbelief and agitation as he recognized the impact of his words.

Chris shook his head. Not so much in reply as to give himself time to absorb the information, or literally to shake it off. Now it was Knollenberg's turn to keep silent. He looked Chris in the eye, seemed minded to pat his arm. His attitude expressed the concern of a friend.

Dudok and Knollenberg, reunited after twenty years. A delicate alliance, held together by a single sentence, a single event, a single word. Miscarriage.

'Was it a planned miscarriage?' Chris spoke in a toneless voice.

'No, Herr Dudok, certainly not. Julia had confided in us that she was pregnant, and that she was eager to have the child — no, it happened spontaneously. She was very sad. She wanted you to know, and she said she would write and tell you.'

Julia Bender, you failed to do that. You did not write. You did not have the nerve. Why? Why could you not tell me?

In spite of everything, Knollenberg went on, she remained in control of the situation. She asked him to call a trustworthy doctor, and to call his wife, but please not to tell anybody else. A healthy woman having a miscarriage was practically an insult to the German Reich, while abortion was a punishable offence. Knollenberg had gone in search of his own doctor, leaving his wife to look after Julia. She had left the next morning. He remembered watching her walk away with her suitcase, and wishing she would flee the country. He had talked to her, tried to persuade her to cross the border into Holland, but she had stayed in Germany. A month later she was back on their doorstep.

Chris and Knollenberg sat in silence, face to face, arms crossed, ambushed by memories.

A child of Julia's, the beginning of a child, a failed attempt. If he had stayed instead of clearing off to Holland it might never have happened. If he had stood up to her, if he had made her come with him.

If, if, if.

He had done none of those things, he had abandoned her — and yet, for three months afterwards his presence had lingered on. It went against all his convictions, clashed with everything he stood for, but he could not help being overcome by the knowledge that he had fathered a child. Not a child, just a first, tentative beginning. Something had grown, in vain as it happened, yet it had grown.

But he was even more affected by Julia's sorrow. She had been very sad, wasn't that what Knollenberg had said? Very sad, about the child, about him too, perhaps, about her brother of course, about everything that had gone wrong. Sorrow attracts other sorrows; once settled in, it gathers a momentum of its own. Before you know it, you are besieged by sadness. Always on the prowl, give it a finger and it'll take a hand, an arm, an entire body. Knollenberg must have comforted her, been absorbed into her despair, put his arm about her.

'Were you able to do anything for her, at the time? How did it happen, were you there, was your wife?'

Chris stumbled over the questions, which he could barely bring himself to utter.

'It was mid February, Saturday afternoon. I was home early from the office, half past three I think it was. It was snowing, already getting dark. I remember the time quite distinctly because there was light in the front-room windows. I went up the steps and let myself in. It was deathly quiet in the house.'

Why this idiotic preamble? What's the matter with him? Why isn't he answering the question?

'My wife was not in the hallway, but I saw Julia standing stock-still by the door to the guest room. At first I didn't notice she was crying, it was only when I went up to her that I saw the tears streaming down her face.'

He paused, not knowing quite how to proceed, and took flight in a comment about the weather and how cold it had been in the house.

'Julia just stood there. And she whispered: 'It's gone, the baby's gone.' Then she said: 'I want Chris, I want Andreas, I want to go home.' I held her in my arms, Herr Dudok, she laid her head on my shoulder and I patted her on the back. But the next minute she was her practical self again. She was far quicker than me to know what to do. That's when I went to fetch the doctor.'

The piano in the bar had been well and truly discovered, and the first boogie-woogie thundered through the lobby. Chris had listened to Knollenberg's story almost on sufferance. Now came the desolation. He could only just tolerate the music, the buzz of voices, this whole absurd situation. But not Julia's plea — 'I want Chris, I want to go home.' Knollenberg should not have said

166

that, he should have left it out.

I want to go home. Primal supplication, a yearning for the time before the terror took over, before the accident of her father and mother. Chris knew. He was the boy lying in the field with his cheek against the calf, staring into the endless sky. He had seen the creature fall. It was near a water trough, where the grass was muddy and trampled by hooves. That time in his life, that sky, his cheek against the dead calf's flank, giving himself up to the sucking void, entering a wondrous vacuum. And his father in the distance.

17

The sun. The light among the trees on the far side of the fen seemed to flicker with lightning. Swathes of dew on the lawn, glistening. A ribbon of mist bordering the small lake, overlaid by the long rays of rising sunshine. Sunday, how apt. An irrevocable day.

Chris Dudok lay back, looking out over the water, registering the gradual changes in the atmosphere. Dominating his view was the sundial in the middle of the garden. From afar it resembled a pair of cupped hands, the fingers splayed to indicate the time in gold and blue, shadow and light. Ungraspable time made graspable. It seemed thus, but was not so.

August 13th: sun-up at 6.28 a.m., sundown at 21.06 p.m. It said as much in his diary.

The sunrise alone mattered to him. The day would be fine. The night was as good as spent, the drowsy hours beneath his rug running out. No paperboy today, thank God. He had taken that into account. There would be nobody coming to the house.

Suddenly he heard a noise, the thud of car doors, raised voices. They were not far away;

disturbingly close in fact. An engine started; he heard the crunch of tyres on gravel — could it be his gravel? Dudok stiffened. Who on earth could be coming up his drive at this hour? The car accelerated, it was just round the corner, who the hell . . . ? He saw the sweep of headlights on the road along the fen, then it was gone. The neighbours, of course! He had forgotten about Lottie and her parents going on holiday.

'I have to be up at six, Meneer Dudok.'

She would no doubt be huddled on the back seat, half asleep, with Mark in her head, Mark Blinkert. What a wonderful name, and what a dear girl she was, that Lottie.

Dudok took a deep breath, his heart was still pounding as he steadied his nerves. He listened to the dwindling sound of the car, how it turned onto the main road and gathered speed, holiday-bound. Would they be heading for France? Italy maybe?

Rome. He could not recall the exact year; he had lost count of the times he had been in Rome since the death of his wife. Always Rome, from there to Naples, then Capri, a fixed itinerary for an unfixed heart. Sometimes with Stoet for company, more often alone. Back in the '60s the three of them had made the trip together more than once. After years of love, Stoet and his wife continued on

169

the same footing as before.

Dudok had endured those years, he had grown accustomed to her dividing her life between Stoet and himself. He had looked the other way, finding it surprisingly easy to do so. Stoet's impetuosity, his wife's resoluteness, and his own — well, his own what? What sort of character trait would fit here? How would an impartial outsider fill in the blank, what was his most salient characteristic, how would it be defined?

Alienation, denial, loss — Dudok, where do you stand, what do you feel? Yearning, that was the correct term, his perennially suppressed, deeply buried sense of yearning. Do you hear what I am saying, Stoet, do you hear?

He had wandered the streets of Rome with Stoet, his friend, the only friend he could put a name to. Late May, warm weather, the evening air as soft as the touch of a hand on his neck. His wife had died a few months previously. Stoet had been the last person she spoke to, but he had made no mention of what had passed between them. He had been staying at their house at the time, and all three of them were aware that she could not last much longer. It had been an episode of complete resignation, a wave rising from a flat sea and rolling inexorably, soundlessly, towards them until the day it halted over their

170

heads and came crashing down.

'What did she say to you, Stoet, at the end?'

He had been waiting for an opportunity to ask that question for weeks. They were dining alfresco on the Piazza Farnese, a square of nigh perfect proportions dominated by a robust palace doing service as an embassy. Few cars, few pedestrians, *carabinieri* standing at ease by the entrance to the building. It was dark, except for the restaurant lighting. The plank floor of their terrace creaked under the waiter's tread; from the Campo di Fiori nearby came the sound of music. It was May 1974, the first spring since her death. The first manifestations of remorse and sorrow and relief.

Stoet hesitated, put down his knife and fork, took them up again, only to put them down beside his plate once more. He glanced around for the waiter, anxious for a refill. Beckoned, made a pouring motion.

'She said I was to keep an eye on you, Chris. That she wanted me to make sure you were alright. Most of what she said was about you. We didn't talk for long, she was too exhausted, well, you don't need me to tell you that. She did say — I couldn't hear very well — she did mention that there had always been something troubling you, some preoccupation you never told her about and which she did not

171

understand. She said that your soul was else-where. Yes, that was what I heard her say, your *soul*, a word I had never heard her use before. She thought it had something to do with the war. She had tried to ask you about it several times, but you always evaded the question.'

Stoet paused, rubbing his forehead. 'She said it used to upset her in the early years, but all that had passed. She respected your secrets, she said. She had a few of her own.'

Chris felt a strong urge to agree, to tell Stoet that he knew all about her secret, and that it had not affected the friendship between the two of them in the least. It had actually given him a measure of freedom. But he said nothing, not wishing to cause embarrassment.

Two boys were kicking a soft-drink can across the piazza, the clatter echoing all around. Stoet kept silent. Chris listened to the trajec-tory of the can as it bounced off into a side street. Then, looking his friend full in the face, he felt the tears brimming from his eyes. The echo of the tin can, the distant music, his dead wife's last words, Stoet taking a large gulp of his wine, the mild evening on the piazza.

He made no effort to check his tears. No-one paid any attention to him aside from Stoet, who stared in frozen wonder at the sight of Chris expressing his emotion so openly — almost thankfully, even.

Looking back, he was mystified as to what precisely had made him weep. An ancient spring had been tapped, a deep well in which no water was surmised, but he had wept as he had not done since boyhood. With reserve, admittedly, inaudibly, unobtrusively. Only one or two people in the crowded restaurant had noticed, and likely as not thought he was shedding tears of laughter. Moist eyes and happiness at a dinner table in the open air. And perhaps it was true, perhaps it was happiness, come as a thief in the night.

His wife had known all the time, or guessed, or at any rate resigned herself. She had sensed his distress on his return from Lübeck, and again all those years later, on his return from the trade fair in Frankfurt. Not that he had ever said anything. But she could tell by his evasiveness, by the faraway look in his eyes, by his absorption in something that was beyond her. So she imagined that he must have been in love with someone else. Who was this person, where was she? In due course that question, too, was subsumed into their shared years and the agonizing ordinariness of their marriage. Their barren communion.

She had married a masterful reckoner, a cool, killjoy mathematician. She had continued to live with him, or with what remained of the man she had fallen in love with, which was enough to ensure her abiding concern for his welfare. She had recommended him to the care of his friend, her friend, her long-ago lover. So many treaties, so much defeat, so much left unsaid. From the Reeuwijk lakes until death, good Lord, was that it? Had nothing happened in between, had there been no glimmer of love at all?

The tin-can boys reappeared from another side street and came running past their terrace, shouting and waving to somebody across the square. At the same instant, both men faced away to watch the boys' movements. Chris quickly patted his face with his napkin.

Back in Rome, back on the piazza, back at the dinner table.

18

He took up his watch, which he had left on the garden table. The rug had slipped to the ground. Dudok pulled it back up over his legs, not on account of the chill this time but to restore order.

The old fob watch indicated seven. Each half hour from now on, he would flip up the lid, inspect the time, and shut it again, his ear cocked to register the refined little click as it locked into place.

His grandfather's watch, not intended for the timing of any kind of finish.

Why keep such a close watch on the time, when it held no further promise? Silly markings, silly pointers on a face of white marble, a small box on a chain. Pointless, superfluous gadget.

He would have to get it over with by ten o'clock at the latest, he had decided.

The lid would flip open another half dozen times. And shut again with six more of those sublime clicks. He had never really noticed the sound before; it seemed to be being picked up by a minute antenna in his chest. A sensation not unlike that of watching a shop girl wrap a parcel with great care, rustling the paper, running her painted fingernail down a fold, snapping the elastic band about the package. A fraction of hypnosis.

Seven o'clock. Still quiet, no cars, no neighbours, no church bells. Plenty of time to get things ready in the kitchen. Should he go upstairs first, to his study? Take the habitual route to his den with all his books, newspapers and company reports? No, rather not. He remained seated, Rome in his thoughts. His mind was clear, he was wholly prepared.

Now for the conclusion. No more groping for images in the infinite space of his memory, as in this past night spent on his terrace. The morning was rising, his hours of reverie lay behind him, his consciousness seemed restored.

Rome.

He looked at the watch: half-past seven. Half-past seven? So he had nodded off again, while he was so sure he had everything under control.

Click. He lay very still; his shiny toecaps poked out from under the rug.

Down the Corso, and then, on the corner of Piazza Venezia, there it was: the Palazzo Doria Pamphili, secret tip for the sophisticated traveller. Fifteenth-century, nothing special by Roman standards. Chris had long wanted to visit the *palazzo*, and Stoet was willing. It was said to be worth the detour, and with reason: handsome apartments of human proportions, rooms one felt directly at home in. Very few visitors, the site was not listed in the standard travel guides. Penetrating further into the building they arrived at the *gallerie*, spacious corridors with four or five tiers of paintings on the walls. There was no order or method to be discerned in the arrangement of the dizzying number of art works, yet one was irresistibly drawn to the next display.

Then he saw her.

Unassuming, unlit by any spotlight, one of the most intimate pictures he had ever set eyes on. Third from the top in the profusion of canvases, a small portrait of a woman. There she was. The artist must have known her well, he must have loved her.

Julia. But also Agatha, Agatha van Schoonhoven, mistress of Jan van Scorel. Portrayed with a depth of feeling that cannot have been other than all-consuming love. He had never seen an original Jan van Scorel before, only reproductions in art books. A portrait dating from 1529, painted yesterday, hung today. Spitting image of Julia. The modesty of her attire — ivory-coloured headdress, dark bodice over a white shift — did nothing to conceal her passion, or his.

Chris stood rooted to the spot, notwithstanding a strong urge to run, as though from a sudden blast of wind, or in answer to the summons of a bell. Notwithstanding Stoet's motioning him to move on.

The very same eyes, in his doorway, her dark woollen hat pulled down over her ears, her honey-blond hair tousled and darkened in the wet. Five a.m. Suddenly there, after having searched for her all night. Reaching out to touch her cheek, feeling her hand covering his. Perhaps love finds its most perfect expression in a gesture. Her hand curved around his hand. The human memory is deeply versed in wordless acts, best at retaining the quiet moments of tentative contact: her hand round his hip, her mouth covering his. The cries in the street faded. It was in those hours that the child —

Knollenberg had known, Chris had not. It had been Knollenberg comforting her, not him. Knollenberg, the man he had suspected of turning a blind eye, of keeping silent, of collaborating and surviving, the man who had helped her, who had given her food and shelter. Knollenberg, the Samaritan. Whereas he had submitted to being dispatched to Holland like a mindless evacuee.

178

The eyes in his doorway on the Muster-bahn, the neoclassicist mansion with columns flanking the entrance — there were her eyes, up on the wall, her eyes beneath a white head-dress, painted from life by a medieval master four hundred or so years ago. Four centuries made no difference, none at all.

Stoet came strolling towards him, tapped him on the shoulder: 'Time for tea, Chris.' Then, pointing to the picture, he quoted from his museum brochure: 'Jan van Scorel, Agatha van Schoonhoven, Utrecht 1529.'

No. Julia Bender, Lübeck 1938.

Tea, should he make a cup of tea? Eight a.m. seemed an appropriate time for tea. He would have to get a move on. It was all going so fast, astonishingly so. The watch-lid flipped open, and shut again, with a regularity that was no longer of his own doing. Whoever failed to rise now would be too late, whoever was alone now would remain so for a very long time.

Why not stay where he was? What was there to stop him?

He would fall asleep, wake up in the afternoon, ring Van Dijk with a simple request: to drive him to a restaurant in town later on. He would invite Stoet to join him for dinner. No, that would be absurd, since the die had been cast. Die. Curiously apt for the occasion: once cast there was no return.

Dudok rose from his chair with effort. Both his Achilles tendons ached, his knees were stiff, his blood was sluggish. He stood upright on legs that preferred the horizontal stance, his shoes pinched, he could barely move his neck. He reached for the doorpost, leaned against it.

Nine a.m. He heard the soft chimes of the clock in the hallway, on the other side of the sitting-room door. He had not caught the sound out on the terrace. Dudok looked about him, greeting the room with his eyes, and was reminded of the poem about Marc, the little boy who 'greets all the things in the morning'. Mark, Lottie's boyfriend. Mark Blinkert: why was he thinking of people he did not even know, had never met.

The kitchen, that was the first order of business. It was a long trek across the sitting room. Past the bulbous-legged table with the pewter dish by the front window. A news-paper lying on the windowsill roused a flicker of interest; he noted a couple of oranges, a leather *etui*, a cigarette case, a pair of sun-glasses, all sharply defined.

No hanging about now, no lingering over every piece of furniture, no contemplation of pictures. No inspection of the fireplace — of course the grate was empty of ash, it was August; nobody was lighting fires; Van

Dijk would not be getting the wood in until October. Just focus on walking to the other side of the room.

Walking was putting it too strongly: he was moving, straggling, advancing a little way, halting, clutching his lower back where it hurt. He shuffled past the drinks table by sofa with the cut-glass tumblers, the bottle of Jack Daniels and the silver bowl for ice cubes, his tread on the parquet making the glasses tinkle. Seeing the whisky bottle brought a vague association to his mind. Take no notice, Chris, just carry on.

He steadied himself against the small bureau with the photograph on top. Familiar face in a dark leather frame. He decided he could afford to sit down for a moment on the chair by the bureau. Five minutes' rest, no more.

His sister. The very antipode of himself, gazing out at him from the leather frame. He both wanted and did not want to look back. His sister. Gracious, life-affirming, dyed-in-the-wool champion of everything he had no faith in. She believed in having children, believed in humanity, believed in God, in a supreme being, a distant kingdom, a mirror whose current murkiness would one day resolve into brilliant clarity. A believer in goodness and beauty, against all the odds. A

Salvationist in mufti.

He laid her portrait face down, gripped the armrests of his chair and pulled himself to his feet. He approached the grand piano in the side room. His wife used to play the piano — quite well, too — but that was a very long time ago. Her musicianship had not survived the war. The instrument looked forlorn; no-one ever played it.

The cover stood open. He slammed his hand into the yellowed keyboard at the low end. A sound like a subterranean drum roll. He moved on to the kitchen.

Slow, slower, slowest, while everything else was speeding up. Notably the time.

19

Upstairs in the study, seated behind his narrow, somewhat ladylike desk — if there was anywhere he was safe, it was there. The morning hit its stride with a swift gathering of heat in the windless air. He had placed the cereal bowl on the right-hand corner of the desk, where it stood in innocent readiness like a belated breakfast.

All set, then. He was no longer in a hurry; all the necessary steps had been taken, nothing had been overlooked. Cooking the oatmeal porridge had not been easy without Van Dijk to guide him. He opened the drawer of his desk and fumbled in the depths for a large brown envelope. The flap was stuck down. Frankfurt postmark, German stamps. On the front: Dr. Chr. Dudok, and the address of the factory, written in a firm hand. Posted on 30 May, 1958. Sender: J. Knollenberg.

J. What would the initial have stood for? Johannes, Jürgen, Justus? He had already seen the contents, long ago. After a moment's hesitation he took his letter opener and carefully slitted the resealed envelope along the top.

The newspaper, plus letter attached with a

paperclip. Dingy, yellowed newsprint, almost crumbling at the touch. German newspaper, Gothic type, irritating to read, aggressive, angular, as though composed of small blades. *Lübecker Generalanzeiger, 2 April, 1942.* Sent to him by Knollenberg. An article describing the air attack on Lübeck, including a list of names of casualties. Those of the previous days, those whose remains permitted identification. He slipped the accompanying note back into the envelope.

'They flew over in the night of March 28 at a little after 11 p.m., wave upon wave of bombers in a raid lasting until 2.30 a.m., sweeping over Travemünde, then back to the Baltic and home to the accursed British Isles . . . '

The first major strike on an irreversible path of destruction. Dudok read; he followed the report in which the journalist reviewed the damage to the various neighbourhoods of Lübeck. In his mind's eye he saw the bombs dropping on the Old Town: Breite Strasse, Meng Strasse, Johannis Strasse, the merchant quarter extending to the harbour. Ribbons of fire, pillars of flames, blazing churches, the Marienkirche, the cathedral, the Petrikirche. There was a photograph with the article showing the Dom and the Musterbahn; he could see the house he used to live in, damaged but still standing. The Musterbahn was where it all started, the first blitz, the first fires, the first showers of sparks spreading the flames. His Musterbahn, their Musterbahn. He could just make out the arched windows of his basement.

Street by street, house by house, the attacks by the Lancasters, Stirlings and Wellingtons were carried out with flawless precision. Palm Sunday, 1942. The Lord entered the city on a donkey, and behold, all was ablaze.

Had she been in her own home?

He stopped reading; he knew the story. In his note Knollenberg mentioned that he had witnessed the raid from his house outside the Altstadt, and that he had gone looking for casualties the following morning. Julia had not been found until several days later. He had kept the newspaper with her name listed among the dead ever since, but was now sending it on to Dudok because 'perhaps it will help you to believe it'.

It had not helped, not that he had doubted the truth of the matter. Without thinking, he drew a thick circle around the list of names in bold type. There she was, tucked in between Hans Aldorf and Albert Benning: 'Julia Bender (aged 31)'. He stared at the name, felt in his waistcoat pocket for his watch. Drew it out, flipped up the lid: close on ten o'clock. Shut it again.

He rested both hands in front of him on the desk, as though sitting down to a meal, which was, in a sense, the case. His right hand lay next to a biro; he picked it up, scribbled a few lines on a loose slip of paper.

The early hours, half-past four, five in the morning, just after the war. The small ferry rocking as he shifted his weight, the mist rising from the canal. To anyone watching from the side he would have been Charon, ferryman of the dead. Chris worked himself across to the factory, dragging the wooden handle along the steel cable with effort.

He lifted the bowl of porridge, placed it in front of him, and took up the spoon.

The huge doors of the factory hall, the *Heyligenstaedt* recovered and reinstalled, the vast space, the chains, the pigeons high in the rafters.

The day, the hour. Now was the time. Now or never. He ate his porridge, one hand resting beside the bowl, the other holding the spoon, elbows off the table.

The pigeons whirring up and away through the awning window.

Dudok sat back and waited. Fifteen minutes, half an hour, then he stood up. Perhaps he should lie down in the bedroom. He set himself in motion. One knee buckled, then the other. Skewing round his axis, he collapsed.

20

The men introduced themselves. Purely
routine, they said; their investigation would
not take long. Just a few questions they
wished to ask Van Dijk. They followed him
upstairs. The last of his anger evaporated as
he pointed the officers to the study, the doorway of which was so imperiously obstructed
by his dead boss.

The police officers stood still on the
landing, the pale figure in his Sunday suit at
their feet. They seemed to observe a moment's
silence as they stood side by side, gazing into
the room. A tribute to the anonymous dead.
Routine? It did not look like it.

Van Dijk was impressed by their grave
composure. They proceeded to step over
Dudok with circumspection; one of them
crouched down by the body, the other went
over to the desk. Then came the questions:
where had he been last night, had he known
about Meneer Dudok's intention, had there
been any hints, any particular instructions?
Had Van Dijk, by any chance, been
dispatched to purchase medicines, had his
boss received any visitors the previous day?

Van Dijk told them, then pointed to Dudok. 'Suicide, as you can see for yourselves. Pills, a fatal dose. The doctor said he must have been saving them up. He said they were from Belgium, he could tell by the label on the box. Someone must have sent them to him, I can't imagine who. And look, there's a note: it's in German, a couple of lines slanting across. The handwriting is Meneer Dudok's.'

Van Dijk indicated the slip of paper lying on the desk. The older inspector peered at it with puzzlement, called to his colleague for assistance. Together they slowly deciphered the German script, whereupon the younger of the two finally read it out with solemn bemusement. *Wer jetzt kein Haus hat baut sich keines mehr, wer jetzt allein ist wird es lange bleiben.* Whoever has no house now will never build one, whoever is alone now will remain so for a long time. The words sounded very strange to them, hard to make sense of. Not what you would call a farewell message, they reckoned.

'Probably fell out of a book,' one of them said, with a nod to the bookshelves lining the wall. Van Dijk made no comment. For some reason he was moved to hear those words intoned in heavily accented German. He did not think Meneer Dudok would have invented something like that; it was bound to

188

be some quotation that had occurred to him at the last. Not much of a farewell, indeed. Not much of a message either.

Wer jetzt allein ist. Whoever is alone now.

Van Dijk went over to the window, one hand behind him, the other raised to his neck. The rustling sounds and murmured conversation at his back were almost gratifying to him. The garden was looking splendid. He would have to do something about that wicker chair, though, it looked somewhat out of shape; Meneer Dudok did not like that. The dry cleaners would be coming round tomorrow, so would the cleaning lady, and the Wolsely had to be taken to the garage.

Daydreams. Fantasies about everything simply carrying on as usual, about the working week starting tomorrow, going to the factory on Wednesday and making an early start to avoid the rush-hour traffic.

A large white van turned slowly into the drive. The ambulance, he realized with a start. What good would that do? Rules, the doctor had said. First the police, then the ambulance.

He turned round. The police officers were collecting their belongings; they had all the information they required. The newspaper remained lying on the desk, half obscured by Dudok's last testament. Van Dijk saw the

189

officers to the door, where he greeted the ambulance drivers. He motioned them to go upstairs, while he went to the kitchen for a breather. He shut the cupboard door, washed the saucepan, took the spoons from the sink and put them in the drawer, heard the stretcher being manoeuvred down the stairs.

Someone issued instructions in an urgent whisper: 'Steady now, keep it straight, gently does it.'

They slotted him into the back of their van without a sound; the driver lifted his hand in greeting as they drove off.

Van Dijk stood on the doorstep, following them with his eyes. He listened to them take the narrow road along the fen. No earthly need for hurry.

Other titles published by
The House of Ulverscroft:

FRANCES AND BERNARD

Carlene Bauer

He is Bernard Eliot, a poet: passionate, gregarious, a force of nature. She is Frances Reardon, a novelist: wry, uncompromising and quick to skewer. In the summer of 1957, Frances and Bernard meet at a writers' colony. Afterwards, he sends her a letter, and with it begins an almost holy friendship. From their first, witty missives to dispatches from the long, dark night of the soul, Frances and Bernard tussle over faith and family, literature and creativity, madness and devotion — and before long, they are writing the account of their very own love story.

We do hope that you have enjoyed reading
this large print book.

Did you know that all of our titles
are available for purchase?

We publish a wide range of high quality
large print books including:

Romances, Mysteries, Classics
General Fiction
Non Fiction and Westerns

Special interest titles available in
large print are:

The Little Oxford Dictionary
Music Book
Song Book
Hymn Book
Service Book

Also available from us courtesy of
Oxford University Press:

Young Readers' Dictionary
(large print edition)
Young Readers' Thesaurus
(large print edition)

For further information or a free
brochure, please contact us at:

Ulverscroft Large Print Books Ltd.,
The Green, Bradgate Road, Anstey,
Leicester, LE7 7FU, England.
Tel: (00 44) 0116 236 4325
Fax: (00 44) 0116 234 0205